THE CALL OF THE SYLVANA

BOOK TWO OF THE SYLVAN CHRONICLES

PETER WACHT

Kestrel
Media Group, LLC

The Call of the Sylvana

By Peter Wacht

Book Two of The Sylvan Chronicles

Published in the United States by Kestrel Media Group LLC.

ISBN: 978-1-950236-02-2

eBook ISBN: 978-1-950236-03-9

Library of Congress Control Number: 2019901433

❀ Created with Vellum

ALSO BY PETER WACHT

THE REALMS OF THE TALENT AND THE CURSE

THE TALES OF CALEDONIA

(Complete 7-Book Series)

Blood on the White Sand (short story)*

The Diamond Thief (short story)*

The Protector

The Protector's Quest

The Protector's Vengeance

The Protector's Sacrifice

The Protector's Reckoning

The Protector's Resolve

The Protector's Victory

TALES OF THE TERRITORIES

A Fate Worse Than Death (short story)*

Stalking the Red Ruby (short story)*

Death on the Burnt Ocean (Forthcoming 2023)

Monsters in the Mist (Forthcoming 2023)

The Dance of the Daggers (Forthcoming 2023)

THE SYLVAN CHRONICLES

(Complete 9-Book Series)

The Legend of the Kestrel

The Call of the Sylvana

* Free short stories can be downloaded from my author website at www.PeterWachtBooks.com.

For Jacob and Michaela.
Thank you for reminding me
about what's really important.

YOUR FREE SHORT STORY IS WAITING

THROUGH THE KNIFE'S EDGE

This short story is a prelude to the events in *The Sylvan Chronicles* and is free to readers who receive my newsletter.

Sign up and get your free copy at www.PeterWachtBooks.com.

1

NEW DIRECTION

Rynlin said it would be just another training session. Thomas hadn't believed him then, and he certainly didn't believe him now. One thing he had learned while living on the Isle of Mist was that Rynlin liked routine. He was comfortable with it, which was one of the reasons why Thomas' day was so regimented. Having a weapons session in the morning struck him as odd, and the fact that Rynlin now watched him with the eyes of a hawk made it meaningful, as his grandfather rarely observed his martial training. Though Rynlin munched calmly on an apple while using the massive root of the nearest heart tree as a seat, the gleam in his eye spoke volumes of his interest in the struggle unfolding before him.

Thomas' grandfather was a tall man, slim but with a deceptive strength. His piercing, green eyes held an intensity that frightened most men and accentuated the sharp features of his face. The short black beard flecked with grey gave him an almost dastardly appearance. If anyone had the courage to tell him so, he would have smiled and thanked them for the compliment.

Rynlin had been back for less than a week, and since then every day offered a new test for Thomas to pass. The previous night, Thomas had again been up past midnight answering questions presented by Rynlin and Rya regarding the Sylvana. The questions came rapidly, with little time to answer. Many times his grandparents spoke over one another, increasing the difficulty. The questions he answered incorrectly yesterday he would have to answer correctly tonight. And if he got them wrong again ... well, he didn't want to think about that. Neither Rynlin nor Rya was known for their patience. Thomas told himself to stop letting his mind wander and instead focus on the task at hand.

Not the tallest of lads, Thomas' constant training had given him broad shoulders and a wiry strength. Pushing several strands of wavy brown hair from his brow, he turned his sharp green eyes to the figures standing across from him. These and the other spirits he fought against during training were brought forth by Rynlin, using in the Talent in a way that Thomas had yet to learn. Usually when he practiced in the ring, he faced one opponent. Today he fought three men known as shock troopers. They were the vanguard of what had once been the army of the Perosian Empire, which for a time had stretched along the western coast of what are now Kashel, Inishmore, and Ferranagh, and included both the Western Isle and the Distant Islands.

The three shock troopers circled him now, moving on their toes. They made him think of the big cats that hunted in the Highlands and how they stalked their prey. The three men wore standard armor with chain mail for the legs and arms and interwoven plates of steel covering their chests, torsos and thighs. What surprised Thomas were the steel helmets. Each one was unique, although they all followed the same theme. Instead of the nose guard or slits common to the Kingdoms, the steel displayed images of ancient monsters. He understood why they were called shock troopers. If an opposing force didn't know what to expect, they would most likely run in terror from these warriors, thinking they were fighting creatures from their nightmares rather than men. The shock troopers twirled small spears in front of them as they circled Thomas, with one end of the blade ending in a sharp spike and the other curving to form the edge of a scythe.

His opponents had watched him for several minutes now, not bothering to attack. Instead, they waited patiently for an opening. Thomas grasped only his sword and a small spear. He was clearly at a disadvantage, yet competing against Antonin and his other weapon tutors had shown him that no matter what the odds, you always had a chance. Thomas watched the movements of his three opponents carefully, turning slowly around in a small circle of his own, trying to keep an eye on the man behind him. He knew the first attack would come from that direction.

The three shock troopers slowly closed the circle, waiting for their chance. They yelled at him now, trying to unsettle him. Their bloodcurdling cries set his teeth on edge. Still, Thomas ignored them. That was the first step in surviving any battle. You had to remain calm and focused. With three opponents, a single mistake on his part would lead to a quick death.

With blazing speed, the trooper at his back launched himself at Thomas, swinging his scythelike spear at Thomas' neck. A well-placed stroke would have taken his head off. Thomas quickly sidestepped the attack and moved behind the trooper. For a brief moment, Thomas was out of the trap, with only one opponent in front of him. Thomas lunged forward, not wanting to waste this opportunity. He stabbed with his spear, taking the trooper in the back of his thigh. With his first attacker's attention focused on the steel in his leg, Thomas sliced with his sword across the man's neck, forcing the blade underneath the dragon-shaped helmet where it met the breastplate. In a flash, the man disappeared, returning to wherever he had existed before Rynlin had called him forth. Thomas had won the first skirmish.

The two remaining troopers immediately took up positions so Thomas was once again turning slowly, trying to watch his front and back at the same time. The minutes passed slowly as he followed the movements of the two men. He wanted to wipe the sweat from his brow, but he couldn't take the chance. He guessed that the third one, the one Thomas had killed, had moved sooner than his two companions had expected. That mistake allowed Thomas to escape for a few seconds. He didn't think he'd have the same opportunity again.

This time the two shock troopers attacked at the same time, one charging forward with his weapon raised high, the other lunging with his weapon low, aiming for Thomas' legs. Thomas let his training and instincts take over. He ran forward himself, toward the trooper with his scythe raised above his head. He wanted to put as much space as possible between himself and the second trooper coming at him from behind.

The trooper in front of him was surprised to see his target charging at him. Thomas saw it in his eyes, but the man recovered instantly and swung his spear in a shorter stroke. Thomas caught the scythelike blade with his sword, then jabbed with his spear. The man dodged Thomas' lunge, but it put him off balance. Thomas didn't let him recover. He kicked out his right leg, slamming into the trooper's knee. The man fell to the ground with a cry of pain. Allowing his instincts to take over, Thomas swung his sword in a broad arc behind him, stopping the blade of the second trooper just inches from his leg. Again Thomas stabbed with his spear, but this trooper was the quickest of the three, and he stepped back easily. The injured trooper remained on the ground, so Thomas left him to focus on the other trooper, a soldier whose mask resembled the dragons of yore.

He continued his attack, swinging his sword and stabbing with his spear, the steel often no more than a blur. But much to Thomas' disappointment, the trooper blocked each of his maneuvers. Thomas was losing time. The injured trooper would be on his feet soon, and then he'd be back where he started, caught in a standoff. Worse, the duel had lasted for more than an hour now, and he was getting tired. Both of his arms ached, and he knew that his movements had slowed. The faster you tired, the sooner you made a mistake. Thomas decided to try a different approach.

He turned quickly toward the second trooper, now rising from the ground. The other trooper saw his opportunity, reversing his spear and stabbing for Thomas' back. Thomas had expected that, and he again twisted around, deflecting the thrust with his spear. He then swung with his sword at an angle. The blade sliced through the shock trooper's armor and the man disappeared. Two down.

Thomas jumped back around, but saw that he had misjudged. The injured shock trooper had gotten up faster than expected and was only a few feet from him, his blade poised to strike. Having no chance of evading the thrust, he did the only thing he could, thrusting with his spear and taking the man in the gut. It was a killing blow, but the trooper's blade struck home too, taking Thomas in his side. The third trooper disappeared.

"A good fight," said Rynlin, rising from his seat underneath the tree and throwing the apple core into the bushes. "You misjudged in the end, though."

"I know," said Thomas, thankful that it had only been a practice session. If it had been a real fight, he would be dead.

"Still, holding off three shock troopers is quite a feat."

"I should have won."

"That may be," said his grandfather. "But you didn't. Next time, make sure you do." Rynlin headed for the house and

Thomas followed, putting his sword in the sheath strapped to his back so he could use his sleeve to wipe the sweat from his brow.

His sword. After all these years it was still hard for him to think of it as his sword. The claymore had belonged to his other grandfather. All the swords that kings or lords wore at their sides had magnificent jewels in the hilt that sometimes ran halfway up the blade. But his grandfather's sword – he corrected himself – his claymore was different. In fact, it looked just like any other claymore that a Marcher might own.

The long, double-edged blade held an air of menace. The hilt was wrapped in soft leather so his hand wouldn't slip. The symbol of the Kestrels – a raptor streaking down from the sky, claws outstretched to grasp its prey – was carved into both sides of the blade and at the pommel and was the only form of ostentation, along with the words "strength and courage lead to freedom." Words that seemed to burrow more deeply into his heart with each passing day.

The strain of the contest, both mental and physical, had exhausted him. Maybe staying alive for as long as he did was a victory in itself. Thomas threw out that notion immediately. If you accepted defeat you wouldn't live very long. That's what Darius the Great had said when teaching Thomas how to fight with a dagger. It was funny, really. Praised as a cunning states-man, the politics of Darius' time involved an unusually high amount of bloodshed. To survive, Darius had mastered the dagger, since it was the best weapon for fighting in tight corri-dors and other places with little room to maneuver. It all related to an earlier lesson that Thomas recalled. In short, people remembered what they wanted to remember. Thomas wondered what people would remember of him, if anything at all.

2

A LITTLE FUN

"**A**re you ready for your next lesson?"

"My next lesson?" asked Thomas, surprised. Thomas smiled for an instant. Perhaps Rynlin would finally teach him how to summon the spirits of the great warriors. He had trained against several, but there were so many more from his history lessons that he wanted to challenge. Rynlin stopped in the glade normally reserved for lessons in the Talent. He should have known. It was only midmorning. Rynlin liked to make the most of his time. Why not fit one more lesson in — or rather test as Thomas saw it — before lunch.

Thomas jabbed the tip of his spear into the ground, then stood next to Rynlin. In the beginning, both Rynlin and Rya had instructed him in the Talent. Thomas would watch how they accomplished a task and try it himself, with either one following along with him to make sure he was doing it right. With time that had changed. Now, they told him to do something, and he had to puzzle it out for himself.

"I've got a simple task for you today. I want you to become invisible."

Simple! Becoming invisible was anything but, requiring a

great deal of skill. Thomas shook his head in frustration. He was tiring of all these tests. Fine, his grandfather wanted him to become invisible. He had some experience in this. He'd do it and offer a little surprise of his own.

Taking a few steps away from his grandfather, Thomas drew in the power of the Talent, the power of nature, enjoying the warmth as it coursed through his body. He then focused the energy inward. In just a few seconds he disappeared. If anyone walked into the glade at that moment, the only person visible would be Rynlin.

"Very good," said Rynlin, looking at where Thomas had been before he had disappeared. "Now why don't you see if you can move around without being detected."

"I already have," replied Thomas, tapping his grandfather on the shoulder. Rynlin jumped, startled at hearing his grandson's voice in his ear.

"Blazes, Thomas! That was completely unnecessary!" he said, his face turning red with anger.

Thomas laughed softly upon reappearing, this time standing right in front of Rynlin. His grandfather almost jumped again, but he controlled himself. That's what you get for trying to teach an impertinent boy. Nothing but trouble.

"I thought it was necessary."

"Why do you say that, Thomas?"

Rya had entered the glade, coming to stand by Rynlin and patting his arm. Rya smiled at her husband's indignant expression. No more than five feet tall, Rya carried herself like a giant. She had the appearance of a queen, her dark chestnut hair regularly slipping down to cover her face, forcing her to sweep it away to reveal her deep blue eyes.

Thomas looked from Rynlin to Rya, then back again. "For the past few days you've tested me at a faster pace than normal — the history of the Sylvana or the Talent or weapons. I want to know why."

They both looked at him with serious expressions. They weren't used to being addressed in such a manner. Thomas held his ground. Things had changed since he returned from the Burren, having taken on and defeated two Ogren to help save a beautiful girl with long black hair -- a beautiful girl who, much to his pleasure and confusion, continued to haunt his dreams. He recaptured his focus. His training had become more intense. As if there was an urgency now that hadn't existed previously. He wanted to know the cause. Rya glanced at Rynlin, who nodded.

"We have been testing you," began Rya, walking to a heart tree and sitting on one of its roots. Rynlin and Thomas followed her, finding their own seats. Heart trees climbed hundreds of feet into the air, their trunks blocking a person's view for a hundred feet to either side. Running along the backbone of the Isle of Mist, the heart trees were thousands of years old. It was said that if you lay your ear against the trunk, you could hear the beating of the earth within it. There weren't many heart trees left, and the same story said that once they were gone, the earth would die as well.

"Why?" he asked.

"Because it was time to see if everything Rya and I have been teaching you had sunk in."

"That still doesn't answer my question."

Rynlin smiled. The boy was sharp. He corrected himself — young man. He, too, sometimes had a hard time remembering that Thomas was no longer a boy.

Rya sighed in resignation. She had always tried to protect Thomas. The trip to the Burren had shown that she couldn't, not anymore. He'd have to protect himself. That's why she'd been so angry for the past week — not because of what had happened in the Burren, though that had not helped her mood; rather life was changing, and she wasn't prepared for it.

"We talked about why the Nightstalker was after you," said Rynlin.

Thomas nodded. The conversation had occurred less than a week before. The sickening stench from what remained of the Nightstalker after Rynlin destroyed it had stayed with him for days. A creation of the Shadow Lord, a Nightstalker towered over a man, easily reaching eight feet in height. Its body the color of black granite and covered in raven black scales, the only way to see a Nightstalker was to look at its head.

Unless it was caught in sunlight, the Nightstalker was invisible, its body automatically adapting to the darkness around it. But you could never miss the eyes, the blood red eyes that glowed in the dark. The sharp white teeth that protruded from its jaws and sharp claws fit its purpose perfectly – to hunt, and to kill. And when given its prey the Nightstalker hunted until it completed its task, no matter how long it took.

"It is true, what I said about the High King most likely wanting you dead so he could take the Highlands for himself. There's more to it, though. I've been speaking with several members of the Sylvana. They, too, think the High King is tied to the Shadow Lord, which means the Shadow Lord wants you dead as well."

Thomas sat on his root without moving, his face betraying no emotion. Maybe it was because he had suspected it all along. Yet, there had to be more to it. Even if the Shadow Lord was allied to the High King, that really didn't explain why the Shadow Lord wanted him dead. He couldn't be that important to the Shadow Lord's plans, whatever they may be.

"Why would the Shadow Lord want me dead?" he asked, still confused. "I can understand that if he's connected to the High King, he would want me out of the way because of my claim on the Highlands. But do you really think he'd waste his time with me, just because I'm a Kestrel? Why not leave that task to the High King? I'm sure he's got plenty of resources, even if they're not as effective as a Nightstalker."

"You're right, Thomas," said Rya, clutching her skirts tightly. She had dreaded this conversation for years, and now that it had finally arrived, she was having a hard time controlling her emotions. "It does seem strange that the Shadow Lord would focus on you." She breathed deeply before continuing, looking at her grandson with sad eyes. His resemblance to their daughter Marya, not only in appearance, but also in attitude, shocked her. "There could be another reason as to why the Shadow Lord would want you dead. One that more directly affects his designs."

How could he affect the plans of the Shadow Lord?

"Are you familiar with any of the prophecies?" asked Rynlin, taking over for his wife. This obviously was not an easy discussion for her.

"Some," said Thomas.

"You know what they are?"

"Yes," he replied with more confidence. "The Seers of Alfeos wrote the prophecies thousands of years ago. They were an ancient order of scholars and mystics who purportedly could predict the future. There are several different prophecies, as the Seers couldn't always agree on specifics, but they're all fairly similar. The problem is, most of the time you don't know what they're referring to until after the fact."

"Correct," said Rynlin. Thomas really did pay attention to his lessons, which was heartening. It made a discussion like this easier. "They always are correct, even if you can't divine it until after the fact. The Sylvana traditionally have studied the prophecies because their primary theme has always revolved around the battle between good and evil. For example, the prophecies predicted the rise of the Shadow Lord. So in the past we've attempted to use the prophecies as a way to determine what the Shadow Lord will do next, where he will direct his next attack."

"Has it worked?" asked Thomas.

"To a certain extent," said Rynlin, leaning back against the trunk of the tree and taking Rya's hand in his own. She had gained control of her emotions at the expense of her skirt. The wrinkles now looked months old. "Trying to figure out what the prophecies mean is always a difficult task since they're so obscure. I have deciphered one thing, though."

"What's that?" asked Thomas, leaning on the edge of the root that functioned as his seat. His stomach growled, but he ignored it. Lunch would have to wait.

"I believe the prophecies speak about you."

3

REVELATION

Thomas stared at Rynlin, too stunned to do anything else. The prophecies spoke about him? His grandfather pushed forward with his explanation, not giving Thomas time to think about it.

"As I said before, the prophecies are very obscure. In order to understand them, you have to know what you're looking for." Rynlin began reciting what sounded like poetry to Thomas.

When a child of life and death
Stands on high
Drawn by faith
He shall hold the key to victory in his hand.

Swords of fire echo in the burned rock
Balancing the future on their blades.

Light dances with dark
Green fire burns in the night
Hopes and dreams follow the wind
To fall in black or white.

THOMAS LISTENED IN DISBELIEF. "Those are the passages that you think apply to me?"

"Yes, I do. As do several members of the Sylvana. Let me explain a little more. Begin with the first line: *When a child of life and death*. When you were born, you had green eyes, which throughout the Kingdoms is recognized as a symbol for life. And any birth obviously symbolizes life. On a sadder note, your mother, Marya, died during your birth."

"That could apply to many people," Thomas protested.

"Yes, it could," said Rynlin. "But I don't think it does. Look at the next line: *Stands on high*. It's a very vague reference. However, it could be speaking about two critical parts of your life. When you become Lord of the Highlands, it has traditionally been known as standing on high. And, when you join the Sylvana, you will be standing on high as well. In fact, you will be standing on the tallest peak in all the Kingdoms. I think the double reference to the Highlands and the Sylvana serves as added confirmation."

"You think I will join the Sylvana?" Thomas' excitement momentarily conquered his rising concern.

"Yes, but we'll get to that in a moment."

"What about the rest of the prophecy? What else applies to me?"

"All of it I think. We just won't know for sure until each event takes place. But I believe the last six lines refer to your battle with the Shadow Lord."

"Wait a second," said Thomas, rising from his seat. "You think that because two lines of the prophecy might apply to me, I'm going to fight the Shadow Lord?"

"Yes," said Rynlin.

"That's absolutely ridiculous. How can you come to a conclusion like that?"

Rynlin held his hands up. "Hold on, Thomas. Let me start over."

Thomas stopped pacing, not realizing he had begun. But he didn't want to sit down. Things were moving too fast. Yes, he knew that he was the Lord of the Highlands, at least in name, and as such, he had certain responsibilities. But this as well? He was supposed to fight the Shadow Lord? It was all just a little too much for him. He was beginning to feel lightheaded, and he realized he had stopped breathing. Taking a slow breath, he told himself to calm down.

"Allow me to explain," said Rynlin. He got up from his seat on the root and began pacing in between Thomas and Rya. He always thought better on his feet.

"Let me repeat the lines of the prophecy that I think apply to you, and I'll give you my reasoning. Admittedly, the prophecies are all very obscure, and we really won't know if you are in fact the Defender of the Light until some later point in time. But, if you are fated to meet the Shadow Lord in combat, then it will happen. There will be no way you can avoid it. That's why I'm telling you this now. I want you to be prepared for that possibility. But I think it's more than just a possibility.

"Also, keep in mind that the prophecies have never been wrong, and though there are several different ones that vary in certain places, they are never very far off when it comes to the important events. For example, all the prophecies correctly predicted the appearance of the Shadow Lord would appear in the world, and that we would defeat him at certain points in time. Now, this is the interesting point." Rynlin was almost jogging up and down between Rya and Thomas. If he kept going at this pace, he'd be three feet below ground before he finished his explanation.

"Before, the result of what would happen was always predetermined, meaning that the Great War was fated to occur, and it was expected that we would successfully push the Shadow

Lord and his Dark Horde back into the Charnel Mountains. Of course, we didn't know this until the Great War ended and we went back to look at the prophecies. Then we were able to decipher what had largely been unintelligible to us before.

"At that time we looked ahead and saw that a battle between the Defender of the Light and the Lord of the Shadow would take place sometime in the near future. Of course, when you're dealing with the prophecies the near future could be a hundred years, two hundred years or more. Anyway, the interesting thing—"

"Frightening thing," said Rya.

"Yes, that's probably the better word. The frightening thing is that that's where the prophecies end. That's as far as the Seers of Alfeos went in their forecasts — to the actual battle between the Defender of the Light and the Lord of the Shadow."

"What do you mean? They stopped seeing the future?" asked Thomas. He had understood everything up to this point, but he still wasn't sure how he fit in to it.

"I mean that the prophecies end during the battle. The seers foretold nothing more beyond that point. They just stopped, and no one can explain why. Listen to the last six lines:

Swords of fire echo in the burned rock
  Balancing the future on their blades.

Light dances with dark
  Green fire burns in the night
  Hopes and dreams follow the wind
  To fall in black or white.

· · ·

"*Swords of fire echo in the burned rock*. That's a clear reference to the last battle, a point that is no longer debated by those who have studied the prophecies, some for hundreds of years longer than I. The battle will take place, and most likely somewhere in Shadow's Reach, or rather Blackstone, as it's known today."

"So the Defender of the Light has to fight the Lord of the Shadow on his ground."

"Exactly, Thomas. Certainly not an auspicious beginning for the contest. Another reference, *Balancing the future on their blades*, gives us a hint to what comes next. The prophecies end with those six lines. Why? Because this battle will determine what will happen next. That's what the last line confirms: *To fall in black or white*. In the past, throughout the millennia since the Shadow Lord came to be, the victor of the battles between good and evil was always foretold. We have always been able to hold back the Dark Horde. But not this time. The result will not be known until the battle is fought. There is nothing telling us what to expect."

"So this battle will determine the future?"

"Yes, it will."

"And if the Defender of the Light loses?" Thomas had a feeling that he already knew the answer.

"Then the Kingdoms have no future at all. The Shadow Lord and his Dark Horde will reign supreme, and humanity will face the possibility of extinction."

It was almost too much for Thomas to take in at one time. His grandfather's argument was logical. Logical enough for Thomas to believe it. A part of him wanted to deny it, hoping desperately that Rynlin was wrong. The attack by the Nightstalker suggested otherwise, however, and he knew that his wish was simply that — a wish.

"And you think I'm the Defender of the Light? Just because a few lines seem to apply to me?"

"Yes, we do." Rya nodded her agreement. "You are a child of

life and death. You are expected to stand on high, at least once, when you return to the Highlands. And it also seems that you may become a member of the Sylvana. If you succeed, at the time you join the Sylvana, you will be standing in the Circle on a rocky promontory that sits atop the highest peak in the Highlands. The highest peak, in fact, in all the Kingdoms, even taller than those in the Charnel Mountains. When you are raised to Sylvan Warrior, much like when you become Lord of the Highlands, it is called standing on high. Another line seems to apply to you as well — *Green fire burns in the night*. You know, as well as me, what your eyes look like when you're angry, and especially during the night."

"I think green fire is a very appropriate description," said Rynlin.

"That may be," said Thomas. "But your argument is still quite flimsy." Why? Why did they have to do this to him? Didn't he have enough to worry about as it was?

"I know," said Rynlin, "but I still think I'm right."

Thomas looked at his grandfather. Rynlin watched him with a quiet intensity. He had never known his grandfather to be wrong, and he didn't think he would come to these conclusions without a great deal of thought. Thomas still wasn't sure if he believed it all himself. Nevertheless, as his grandfather said, it was better to be prepared for the future, rather than surprised by it.

"When will I know if I'm the Defender of the Light?"

"You will know when you know."

"That doesn't help me very much," said Thomas, irritated by the response. "You sound like a Seer of Alfeos."

Rynlin had responded to some of his questions during his lessons in much the same way, and it had never failed to get under his skin. He didn't like asking a question and then not getting an answer. He wanted to know. It's what he didn't know that bothered him, because just like in a battle, that's often what got you killed.

"Rynlin probably didn't give you the best response he could have," said Rya, rising from her seat and patting her grandson on the shoulder. "We don't know if you are the Defender of the Light, but all the evidence points in that direction. The Shadow Lord is stirring. When will the battle take place? We don't know. It could be a year. It could be five years. It could be more. We do think, though, that when the time for that battle arrives, you will be the one in Blackstone, fighting for the future of the Kingdoms."

"No pressure at all, really," joked Thomas. It was the only way he could respond without laughing hysterically. His mind was a jumble of conflicting emotions as he struggled to grasp what he had just learned.

4

A CALLING

R ynlin laughed and came to stand by his grandson too, slapping him on the back. "None at all."

"So we won't know if I will be the one until some time in the future."

"That's correct," said Rynlin.

"Well, there's no point in worrying about it now," said Thomas, sighing. Nothing ever was easy in life, and his only seemed to be getting harder with each passing day. "I've got enough to worry about as it is." If he tried to take in everything his grandfather had told him all at once, he'd probably lose his mind.

"Your obligation to your father's family?" asked Rynlin.

Thomas nodded. "To my other grandfather," he said. "Not to my father's family. My father's family wanted nothing to do with me. I promised Talyn during the fall of the Crag that I would return to the Highlands and retake what belonged to him; belongs to me now, I guess. It's kind of funny. I'm doing it because of my grandfather, and because of who I am, yet no one except my grandfather cared about me when I was growing up there. I've got to do this for people who thought something was wrong with me, like I was tainted, and now I'm supposed to help them."

Rya listened to her grandson. She was proud of him, prouder than he would ever know, and not because of his ability with the Talent or some other skill. She was proud of him because of the person he had become.

"A strange world we live in," said Rynlin. "This is what's bothering you, having to do that?"

"Only in part," said Thomas. His life had just become immeasurably harder thanks to his grandparents. He was tired of carrying everything by himself. If his grandparents could burden him with these additional responsibilities, he felt the need to be rid of some others. There was no better time then now.

"Sometimes I dream about my mother." Thomas walked a short distance away from Rynlin and Rya, gathering his thoughts. He didn't want to hurt them by talking about his mother, their daughter, but he had to. It was the only way to explain.

"I know she died when I was born, but I can see her clearly in my dreams — the sharp green eyes, the dark brown hair. I know it's her." As Thomas described Marya, an ache formed in Rynlin's throat. It happened every time he thought of his daughter.

"Dreams are very powerful," said Rya. "More powerful than most people know. The world of the living and the world of the dead are clearly segregated when we are awake. When we sleep, and we dream, the borders of the two sometimes mesh, and spirits can walk in your dreams."

"What was Marya saying to you, Thomas?" Rynlin was intensely curious. He wanted to know if it had anything to do with what they were discussing. He was certain of what he just said, that Thomas was the Defender of the Light, or at least would be. Some added confirmation never hurt.

"She keeps calling to me, saying that I must do something. She's always standing a long way off, beckoning to me with her hand, as if I'm supposed to follow her. Whenever I see her, I feel as if I'm missing something inside." He pointed to his chest with his hand to emphasize his point. "At first I thought it was the fact that I don't have a mother. That would be the simplest explanation. Now I'm not so sure. It's more like I'm not complete as a person, and the hole that's there remains when I wake. The only time I feel it filling up is when I use the Talent and draw on the power of nature. That's when I feel complete. But as soon as I let go of it, I feel empty again."

"Do you follow her?" asked Rynlin.

"I try to, but I can only take a few steps. She disappears and then I'm standing in this huge valley of long green grass with mountains all around."

Rynlin looked at Rya and saw confirmation in her eyes. He knew what this was about, and it did apply to the prophecies very much in the way Rynlin had expected.

"When you're in the valley, do you see anything else?"

"Yes, a unicorn. A black unicorn, in fact."

"What is the unicorn doing?" he asked.

"Calling to me, as if he's waiting for me."

"How often do you have this dream?" asked Rya.

"Almost every night," he replied. "At first it was once or twice a month, as I mentioned before. For the past few weeks it's been every night and much more vivid than in the past. When I wake up in the morning, I have an intense impulse to find this valley. I know I can find it. All I have to do is start walking, and eventually that's where I'll end up. But I've resisted it so far. Isn't that kind of strange?"

"Actually, it makes perfect sense," said Rynlin. He smiled broadly.

"Then what does it mean?" asked Thomas in exasperation.

"Thomas," said Rya, giving her husband a sharp look, "please ignore your grandfather. He's not very good at explaining things sometimes. It must have something to do with his age. They say the brain begins to go after a time."

"What?" asked Rynlin, confused.

"Rynlin," said Rya. "Please be a dear and let me explain now. Things will move along at a much faster pace."

Rynlin went back to the tree root and sat down in indignation.

"Thomas, it's time for you to join the Sylvana. That's why in the last few weeks we've been spending so much time going over the history of the Sylvana, and a few other things that relate to them."

"It's time? How do you know?"

"I know because you know, in your heart of hearts, that that's what you should do." Rya took hold of his hand and made him sit down next to Rynlin, who gave his wife an angry scowl. She simply ignored him. "That's how it's been done, ever since the Sylvan Warriors first came together. The people who were chosen would see a unicorn in their dreams. The dreams would appear more and more often, until they occurred every night. As the frequency of the dreams increase, so does the urge to go to the valley where the unicorns reside. Now it's time for you to go. If you hadn't told us about the dream, in a week, maybe less, you would be on your way to the valley by yourself."

"That would have been a problem," said Rynlin, "because then we'd have to find you."

"So that's how you know? The dreams?"

"Yes," said Rya. "They will inexorably pull you to the Valley of the Unicorns so you can overcome the challenges."

"The challenges? What challenges?" Thomas was extremely tired of tests.

"You don't have to worry about those yet," said Rynlin. "We'll tell you more about them when we get to the Circle."

"When will we be going?"

"In a few days," replied Rya. "We need to give the other Sylvan Warriors time to arrive before us. Some are likely already on the way."

Thomas sighed again. His life was becoming more difficult.

"You know, I can tell you one thing that might help you," said Rynlin.

"What's that?" asked Thomas.

"I believe that you will pass the challenges, and when you stand on the mount, you will know then for a fact whether you are the one who will fight the Shadow Lord."

"Well, at least that will answer one of my questions." Thomas was both excited and fearful. Joining the Sylvana had long been one of his hopes. He wasn't sure he wanted to know if he was the Defender of the Light. To be honest, he really didn't want the added responsibility.

"Yes. Then again, the Shadow Lord will know for a fact that it is you as well. Up until now, he has only guessed that it will be you. He hasn't known for sure. That's why only one Nightstalker was looking for you. Once he is certain of his challenger, he will likely take several more steps to remove that threat from the game before it's time to begin playing in earnest."

"Wonderful. Just wonderful. You certainly know how to make someone feel better." Thomas got up from his seat on the tree root and walked toward the house. It had been a long day already and he was hungry. He could worry about all of this after lunch.

"He will have a difficult time with all of this," said Rya, watching her grandson go.

"Yes, he will. But we will be there to help him, as will others."

"At least one thing is certain."

"What's that?" asked Rynlin. He knew what that expression on Rya's face meant. It was the same one she wore when she rode into battle during the Great War — a look of determination, and purpose, that would not be denied.

"With everything Thomas must do, if anyone can handle it all, it is he."

5

———

A NEW SKILL

"Are you ready?" Rya settled her dark blue cloak around her shoulders and stood by the door, tapping her foot impatiently. Thomas' anticipation of the coming journey increased as the appointed time for leaving drew closer. His grandparents now felt much the same way. Outwardly, they remained calm, but as the last few days had passed, their normal reserve disintegrated, exposing the nerves beneath. "And don't forget your cloak."

A biting cold covered the Isle of Mist, a cold foreign to the early fall, a cold reminiscent of darker times. Rya's instincts as a grandmother were out in full force this morning. She insisted that Thomas dress warmly. He wore his brown woolen breeks and a heavy linen shirt, and over that a dark green cloak.

"As ready as I'll ever be." He kept the irritation from his voice, knowing it would only antagonize his grandmother. Thomas had barely slept the last few nights, the excitement of what was to come getting the better of him. The excitement, and the worry. What challenges lay before him? None of the history books explained exactly how you became a Sylvan Warrior, and Rynlin and Rya repeatedly evaded his questions. Their uncharacteristically tight-lipped behavior worried him.

"You'll see when we get there," Rynlin had said, giving him a slap on the back that was supposed to offer some comfort. "You worry too much, you know. You shouldn't worry so much at your age. You'll do just fine."

He worries too much. What a remarkable discovery. Of course, Rynlin didn't appreciate the sarcasm buried within his response. Maybe he did worry too much. Then again, why shouldn't he?

Just three days before his grandparents confirmed that not only did the High King want him dead — something that Thomas had guessed at for years — but perhaps an even greater danger as well. The Shadow Lord. The greatest evil known to the Kingdoms. An evil that gained strength through the millennia while the Kingdoms weakened. And now he wished to become a Sylvan Warrior, if he could overcome the dreaded challenges, of course, whatever those challenges might be.

For the hundredth time he wondered why he wanted to join the Sylvana. Why not find a quiet place and live his life in peace, throwing off the shackles of his responsibilities? Why not forget about the Highlanders? They certainly had no use for him when he was a child. Why not run and hide from the Shadow Lord and avoid any possibility of having to confront him?

Just thinking about that potential confrontation made his blood run cold. No matter how much he thought of that option, he couldn't bring himself to run away. And his grandparents wondered why he worried so much.

"Good. Then let's get going." Rya pushed him out the door and pulled it closed behind her. Rynlin waited for them outside, his dark gray cloak pulled tight around him. Rya was right. It was getting colder. Colder than it should be at this time of year. A light snow from the night before colored the ground white. It created the impression of serenity and peace. On the inside Thomas was anything but.

"Are you ready, Thomas?" asked Rynlin with a smirk. Because of the cold, Rya insisted that her husband wear a hat. He refused, of course. He didn't like hats. As a result, she had spent much of the past hour muttering about how someone's stubbornness would eventually be the death of him. Rynlin tried to ignore her, but disregarding Rya proved difficult on the best of days.

Thomas nodded his assent, catching a glimpse of a black streak bounding into the forest around his home. Beluil, the large black wolf with a band of white across his eyes, sensed that his friend would be away for a while. So he had wished Thomas well before heading deeper into the Shadowwood. The Isle was his home, and though safe because of the terrifying, often haunting stories spread by Rynlin over the years, the large black wolf still liked to make certain nothing encroached on his territory.

"Good. Then it's time to go. Everyone should be there by now."

An impatient man by nature, Rynlin wanted to get this over with, perhaps even more than Thomas. There were too many loose ends right now and his efforts at deciphering the prophecies left him at his wit's end. Combined with the early cold, a cold that reminded him of a dangerous and frightening past, he felt a renewed urgency to find some answers. Once Thomas reached the Circle, Rynlin would know more.

If his grandson failed, then he and Rya were wrong, and Thomas could live a relatively normal life, at least for a few more years until he returned to the Highlands. If Thomas overcame the challenges, though, as both he and Rya thought he would, the course of history would change. For good or bad, he didn't know. And then, for Thomas, becoming Lord of the Highlands would be the least of his worries.

"Before we go, Thomas, we have one more lesson for you," said Rya.

Another lesson? After the past few weeks Thomas thought his lessons had come to an end, at least for the time being. He wasn't surprised, though. Both of his grandparents had a knack for trying to cram as much knowledge into him as they could.

"It's not what you think, Thomas," said Rynlin, seeing the expression on his face. "This lesson is one of convenience. The Circle and the Valley of the Unicorns sit at the edge of the Highlands in a spot that's exceedingly difficult to reach by foot. With this lesson, we'll arrive at the Circle later today. In fact, I think you'll rather enjoy it."

A lesson that he would enjoy? Most, if not all, involving the Talent were arduous at best in the beginning. He surmised that Rynlin really was in a rush to get there.

"Now, Thomas, watch your grandfather," said Rya, patting him on the shoulder. "Pay attention to what he does and how he does it."

Rynlin walked to the other side of the clearing. A sudden surge of energy in the air alerted Thomas that Rynlin had taken hold of the Talent. A white nimbus quickly took shape around his grandfather. Thomas deciphered his shape within it, but as the white light grew brighter, and then brighter still, Rynlin was no longer visible. There was only a pulsating ball of white energy. Whatever his grandfather was doing, it required a great deal of control and strength.

Thomas turned away, shielding his eyes with his hand. He couldn't watch it anymore. The rhythmic white glow was too bright. Just as quickly as the ball of energy formed, it disappeared, the bright white light replaced by the dim glow of the early morning sun. Thomas looked on in shock. Where Rynlin had once stood, a massive hawk had taken his place. The bird shrieked triumphantly, flexing its wings and letting the rays of sunshine glance off its dark brown feathers.

A neat trick, don't you think, said a voice in Thomas' head. It sounded just like the gravelly voice of his grandfather.

"Rynlin?" he asked hesitantly, directing his words toward the hawk, which flexed one sharp claw, and then the other.

The voice returned to Thomas' head. *You shouldn't be so surprised, Thomas. How else did you think we were going to make it to the Circle on time? Flying is the only way.*

"I hadn't really thought about it," he replied, and wondered if the hawk that was his grandfather could understand. The squawk of what sounded like laughter confirmed that he could. "You can shapechange, too?"

"Of course I can, Thomas. As can you. Did you see how Rynlin accomplished it?"

"I think so," said Thomas. "After he pulled in the Talent, he directed it inward, on himself, rather than outward. He focused the Talent on the image that he had created in his mind, the image of a hawk."

"Very good, Thomas," said Rya with pride. He really was a smart boy, when he wanted to be.

The hawk standing before them squawked angrily, gesturing with its head to the sky.

"All right, you old bird. Just hold on." After all these years, you'd think he'd learn at least a little patience. "I'm sorry, Thomas, but it looks as if your grandfather, despite the change in appearance, remains the same grouchy old man we know and love." The hawk squawked in indignation, flapping its wings in anger. Rya ignored the display. "Watch what I do, just to make sure you have it right, then it's your turn."

Thomas nodded and backed away from his grandmother. He again felt the power of the Talent flow all around him. A white nimbus formed around his grandmother, which like the one before grew brighter and brighter. Again the brightness forced Thomas to look away. In a matter of seconds, the white light disappeared and two hawks stood in the clearing, though the one that was his grandmother was the smaller of the two.

Your turn, Thomas. Just do exactly what we did and you won't have any problems. Rya's voice played through his mind, followed by what felt like a mental hug. Even as a bird, his grandmother remained the same.

Thomas looked from one hawk to the next, studying each one closely. He saw some resemblance to his grandparents within those animal shapes, primarily in the eyes. Rynlin's were hard and flinty, while Rya's were warm with a slight edge to them. It was a remarkable transformation.

Still astounded by what he saw, Thomas closed his eyes and locked away everything going on around him, even ignoring the two large birds that were his grandparents. He took hold of the Talent, the rush of energy within his body familiar, and slowly drew in more and more, until he had as much as Rynlin had gathered before he shapechanged. Following the examples of Rynlin and Rya, Thomas formed an image in his mind of the shape he hoped to assume. He then directed the power he held into that image, slowly at first, and then faster and faster until everything he held was used.

Thomas opened his eyes. He was now the same height as his grandparents and looking directly into the eyes of the two hawks. Either he had knelt down or it had worked.

An excellent choice, Thomas, said Rynlin. *The raptor suits you.*

The raptor? He was a raptor? Tipping his head down, the sharp beak where his nose used to be surprised him, along with the white feathers of the underbelly taking the place of his clothes and the sharp claws that served as his hands. He *had* become a raptor. It had worked!

Of course it worked, Thomas. Why are you so surprised? asked Rya.

Thomas quickly realized that in this shape, both his grandparents could read his thoughts, and he could read theirs. He picked up that his grandmother was proud of him because he had gotten it on the first try, and his grandfather was simply irritated, wanting to be on his way. Thomas would have to be careful with his thoughts since this now functioned as their form of communication. It was an intriguing new ability, but then again, knowing someone could read your mind unsettled him.

Don't worry, Thomas, said Rynlin. *We can only read what you want us to read.* He had sensed his grandson's discomfort.

I had the image of a hawk in my mind. Why did I become a raptor?

That's the way the Talent works, Thomas. At least in this respect, said Rynlin. *The Talent shaped itself based upon your personality. For us, the hawk is more appropriate. For you, the raptor. A symbol of the Highlands and the Kestrels. Now, on to more important matters. Let's be off.* Rynlin leapt into the air with his strong legs, the flap of his wings carrying him upward.

Don't worry, Thomas, said Rya, feeling Thomas' worry. *In a very real sense you are now a bird. Flying comes naturally to you. You have nothing to learn. Just allow your instincts to take over.* Rya then leapt into the air, a few flaps of her wings pulling her higher. She soon reached Rynlin, who circled impatiently in the sky high above the clearing.

Since his grandparents had left him on the ground with little in the way of instruction, Thomas had little choice but to follow. Taking a breath, he dug his claws into the soft earth, then pushed off with his legs and flapped his wings. In seconds he was in the air, headed right for Rynlin and Rya, the glade shrinking as he climbed higher. He was flying! He was actually flying! Thomas pumped his wings, gaining altitude rapidly. Shooting past his grandparents, he pushed himself toward the clouds, caught in the exhilaration of it all.

Thomas, now is not the time for games. Come back down here, Rya insisted.

Thomas knew her tone quite well, a tone that brooked no argument. Still, he was several hundred feet above his grandparents, and he could see the sun shining off the waves of the Sea of Mist. The channel separating the Isle of Mist from the Highlands was just off to the west, the mountains of his homeland rising up to meet the sky. Off to the east, the sea dipped off into the horizon. Thomas tilted his body to the right and allowed his extended wings to catch a downdraft. Slowly he turned in a lazy circle until he settled in next to his grandparents.

Please don't do that again, Thomas. The edginess in Rynlin's voice was obvious. When he thought it was time to go somewhere, he didn't like anything to get in his way. *We have a long way to go today, so stay with us. We don't have time for games.*

Sorry, Rynlin.

Don't worry about it, Thomas. Your grandfather is just getting into one of his moods. I think it has something to do with his age.

Rya!

Oh, shush, Rynlin. You said yourself we don't have time for this.

Rya came out of her own circle and turned toward the Highlands, her long, graceful wings catching the wind and carrying her to the far shore. Rynlin followed after her, almost sheepishly. She certainly did know how to put her husband in his place. Taking one final look at the Isle of Mist from his perch in the sky, Thomas followed after them.

6

AN UNEXPECTED VISITOR

As the land passed beneath him at a dizzying pace, the strong mountain gusts pushing him swiftly between the peaks, he marveled at what lay before him. It was an unforgettable experience. The previous night's snowfall blanketed the upper passes and mountaintops with several inches of white powder, while the lower elevations only received a dusting.

Following his grandparents over one mountain plateau, a flash of movement caught his eye. Focusing his sharp gaze in that direction, he picked out the source — a rabbit scurrying for its burrow, frightened by the three predators above it. Upon seeing the rabbit, Thomas felt the immediate urge to dive for the kill. It took all of his will to suppress the instinct. He quickly realized that certain natural instincts of the raptor were now his own, in addition to his ability to fly.

Rynlin, when we are in these forms, do we actually become birds of prey?

What do you mean, Thomas?

Well, Rya said that I didn't have to learn how to fly, because I already knew. I just had to let my natural instincts take over. Does that apply to other things as well, such as having the urge to kill a rabbit if I'm hungry?

In a way, yes. Thomas heard the wheels spinning in Rynlin's head as he formulated an answer. *You see, Thomas, all animals — including man, of course —are very much the same. They have many of the same needs, such as eating and sleeping and so much more. Those traits have simply been adapted to each species. If a hawk is hungry and it sees a rabbit, and a man is hungry and he sees a deer, you'll see much the same in terms of a response. That applies to other things as well. Now, as a man, if you saw that deer, you'd kill it with an arrow, perhaps.*

If you were a hawk, you would use your talons on a rabbit. But both would be giving in to the same instinct. When you took on the shape of the raptor, the image was — what's the best way to say this — placed on top of your own image as a man. It's an awkward explanation, but do you understand? Your dominant shape right now is that of a raptor. Therefore, your dominant instincts will be those of a raptor as well. Because the power to do this came from nature, the instincts and knowledge of that image came with it. And they were placed on top of your own. That's why you had the urge to go after the rabbit, and why if you caught it, you'd be more than satisfied with the meal.

An excellent explanation, said Rya. *Though a bit tedious.*

Don't you think you've given me enough grief during the past few hundred years, woman?

Certainly not, she replied. Rya laughed softly to herself. It was so easy to tease her husband sometimes.

I had one other question, interrupted Thomas.

Why don't you let Rya answer it, said Rynlin in a huff. *I wouldn't want to go on for too long.*

All right. I just wanted to know what happened to our clothes when we changed shape.

I can't say, said Rya sheepishly. *No one has ever figured it out.*

All I know is that when we change back we'll be fully clothed. How was that, Rynlin?

It stands to reason you'd get the easy question.

Oh, don't be such a sourpuss. Just because you're old doesn't mean you have to be grumpy all the time.

Old! Who are you calling old? You're the same age as me.

Yes, but I've retained a youthful outlook on life and have aged much more gracefully—

Thomas decided to fly on his own for a time, so he drifted behind his grandparents several hundred feet. Their favorite pastime, besides making his life difficult, was bickering, and they were very good at both.

The silence, except for the rushing of the wind across his feathers, appealed to Thomas. The gusts of wind curling off the Highland peaks made for a bumpy ride. Much of the time a sudden gust of air pulled Thomas to the left or right. Some even came straight down in bursts, forcing him toward the earth. Despite the constant struggle, he enjoyed every minute of it. Once he learned the rhythm and play of the winds, he focused on the mountains below.

When using the Talent to search, he had done much the same thing as he was doing now, gliding across the earth and looking down at it from a bird's eye view. But this was different. Actually flying above the earth as a raptor added an excitement to it unavailable when he applied the Talent. His grandparents had told him to stay with them, but how was he supposed to have any fun flying behind them as they continued to bicker about the same things they'd been irritating each other with for the past hundreds of years?

Giving in to his desire to explore, he darted away and skimmed low over a mountaintop, marveling at the tough Highland flowers pushing their way through the thin layer of snow in an effort to absorb the sun's warmth. As he circled around another mountain, he flew so close to the tops of the evergreen trees he could have reached out with his talons and snatched the top branch. Soaring through the air made him forget his worries for a time. He reveled in the freedom of it all, shrieking in triumph as he coasted low over a hidden valley then pumping his wings furiously to gain enough altitude to avoid a fast-approaching mountain.

He flew down the other side, spying a herd of mountain goats munching lazily on the sparse grass. He shrieked again, which woke the herd and initiated a mad rush for cover. Thomas almost missed a stroke of his wings when another shriek echoed his own. Tilting his head to the left, he saw that he was not alone. A raptor flew to his right. Thomas banked to the left to catch a warm updraft that would take him to greater heights. The other raptor followed, never more than a few feet away.

It was like he was looking in the mirror, with the white feathers speckled with grey on the underside, orange, brown and black feathers on the back. Thomas guessed the raptor beside him was a female, as it was slightly smaller. At first he thought the other raptor simply wanted to examine this visitor more closely. Raptors were solitary creatures with distinct ranges of territory. Most did not like it when unwanted guests appeared.

Thomas' sharp eyes picked out the two hawks that were his grandparents, at the moment mere specks in the sky. They were probably still arguing. If the raptor thought to defend her territory, she would have attacked already, and with no warning. In fact, Thomas probably would never have known what hit him. Looking over at the raptor flying so closely at his side, something clicked in his mind. Recognition of some sort? This bird seemed familiar, as if he'd seen her before.

The female raptor gazed at Thomas, her eyes seeing

through the Talent at the man beneath. It knew him. How, he couldn't explain, but the female raptor knew him. Could it be the same one he had seen so many times before at the Crag? He always assumed that that particular raptor made the Crag and its surrounding territory its home because it was a good place to hunt. Maybe it stayed for another reason.

For several minutes they flew, the two raptors side by side, never separated by more than a few feet. Thomas glanced over at the other raptor several times. The recognition of who he was remained, and with it was a feeling of approval, and pride. Then, with a squawk of farewell, the smaller raptor tipped its wing and turned back the way it had come. Abruptly, Thomas felt a sharp sense of loss, as if something precious had been taken from him.

Thomas, what have you been up to? He heard his grandmother's words, though they came from a great distance.

Nothing, he replied.

Well, if you don't mind, I'd appreciate it if you'd join us. We're almost there. Rya sounded put out. Rynlin must have gotten under her skin during the bickering. It was just one of his grandfather's many talents.

I'll be right there. Thomas increased the stroke of his wings, straining for more altitude. The higher you were, the stronger the wind currents. You could go farther faster and not have to expend as much energy. He was soon several hundred feet above his grandparents and gaining on them quickly.

There. The two hawks were just below. If they were almost there, it meant it was time to get serious. A lot was riding on his shoulders, placed there by both himself and his grandparents. Well, that didn't mean he couldn't have just one last bit of fun.

Drawing his wings into his sides, he tilted his body downward. He quickly picked up speed as he hurtled toward the earth. The rush was incredible. He had never experienced anything like it before. As the two hawks grew bigger, Thomas adjusted his positioning slightly. In a blur, he streaked past Rynlin and Rya no more than ten feet in front of them. The two hawks halted their flight in surprise, squawking angrily.

Thomas, that was the most childish thing you have ever --

Oh, leave the boy alone, Rya. He was just having a little fun.

Thomas was right. Rynlin had gotten a few of his own zings in during their argument. That was the only thing that could explain his grandfather's magnanimity. He had expected a tongue-lashing from both, but it would have been worth it. Rya bit back her words and they flew on in silence for several more minutes to the northwest when both Rynlin and Rya began climbing higher, reaching for a greater height. Thomas followed their example.

Thomas knew that several of the tallest mountains in the Highlands rose several leagues from tip to base. But the ones they neared exceeded even that. These mountains were immense, dwarfing everything around them. He and his grandparents continued to push for more height, until finally they leveled out. The trees below them were no more than a mass of green now separated from time to time by the whitened tip of a mountain. Rynlin led them over the towering peaks, much of their size hidden by the clouds that formed around their sides.

After they passed the first few, Rynlin angled downward, with Thomas and Rya following. One peak stood out from those surrounding it, rising almost a league higher than any of the others. It was the tallest mountain Thomas had ever seen. It must be the tallest in the Highlands, and probably the tallest in all the Kingdoms.

You're absolutely correct, Thomas, said Rya, reading his thoughts. *It's all of those. It's Athala's Forge, where the Sylvana first gathered.*

Are we going there now, asked Thomas, excited by the possibility, and afraid.

No, not yet. We'll make camp for the night and go to the Circle tomorrow. You'll need your rest to overcome the challenges.

The challenges. He had forgotten about that during the past few hours. His worry returned in a rush.

7

THE CIRCLE

The next morning Thomas woke at dawn. The cold turned his breath to a white mist as he rolled out of his blankets. Rynlin and Rya had already started cooking breakfast over the small fire. Bread and porridge. Something that would stick to his bones, as his grandmother liked to say. As he walked to a nearby stream to wash the sleep from his eyes, his feet crunched softly in the hardened snow. Brushing the frigid water into his scraggly hair, he remembered the discussion from the night before.

When Rynlin landed in the small glade, he and Rya showed him how to change back to his normal shape. Thomas immediately realized just how exhausting shapechanging was. Every muscle in his body felt weak, and he couldn't even stand up straight. He kept swaying from side to side as his muscles twinged and spasmed, protesting what he had just done.

"The more difficult a thing you do with the Talent, the harder it is on you physically," Rya reminded him. "And changing your shape is one of the most taxing things you could ever do with the Talent. But don't worry, dear, the more you do it, the easier it will become, and the less of a burden it will be.

Before you know it, changing shape and flying across the Highlands will take no more of your energy than searching."

Thomas simply nodded during his grandmother's explanation. He didn't have the strength to do anything else. He was having a hard enough time just keeping his eyes open, though it was still only early evening. He watched in a dreamy haze as Rynlin set up camp and got a fire going while Rya prepared a vegetable stew for the evening meal. The ingredients came from the small bag of supplies she always carried with her. The bag at her hip was truly remarkable, mused Thomas. No larger than a small sack, it never grew bigger even though Rya continued to pull out vegetables and cooking supplies.

Thomas had hoped to go to sleep early, but not this night. For the next few hours, his grandparents reviewed everything Thomas had ever learned about the Sylvana, as well as a few things that slipped through the cracks of his memory during his lessons. At first flying seemed like the most exhausting thing he had ever experienced, until now. Even after covering the entire history of the Sylvana, Rynlin and Rya weren't finished. They then told him about each Sylvan Warrior he could expect to meet at the Circle, providing Thomas with a brief description so he would recognize each one.

Later, with the moon halfway across the sky, his grandparents finally let him curl up beneath his blankets by the fire. Unfortunately, his brain refused to turn off and the evening's events played repeatedly through his mind. When he finally fell into a restless slumber, it seemed as if only minutes had passed when his grandfather shook him awake and pushed him off in the direction of the stream. They would leave for the Circle within the hour.

After clearing his head as best he could — the cold water could do only so much — and wolfing down some bread and cheese along with his porridge, Thomas walked to the other side of the clearing to think as Rynlin and Rya cleaned up their small camp. Today's events, regardless of the outcome, would have a tremendous effect on his life. When he left the Crag, his only desire was to survive, to make it out alive so he could fulfill the promises he made to his grandfather. He never expected to find a home, one in which he felt comfortable and safe. After today, unless he failed, he doubted he would ever have that feeling of security again. His life was about to change dramatically, yet for the good or bad he didn't know.

"Thomas, it's time to go."

Rya placed a hand of support on her grandson's shoulder. Rynlin stood in the middle of the glade, their travel bags slung over his shoulder, a confident smile brightening his normally forbidding appearance. His grandfather really must be worried about him. It was the only way to explain Rynlin smiling so early in the morning.

"Remember what we talked about yesterday and you'll do fine," said Rynlin, trying to keep Thomas' spirits up.

Thomas nodded and followed his grandparents into the trees. The air was crisp and cold, helping him gather his wits. He tried to clear his mind of everything except what he was about to do, but he failed miserably and his worries returned tenfold. Would he succeed? Would he overcome the challenges? Could he become a Sylvan Warrior? And if he did, what would happen next? Each worry multiplied into more until Thomas could no longer keep track of them all.

They followed a small, dirt trail that led up a slight incline. The trees pushed in on both sides, forcing Thomas to dodge the branches Rynlin held out of the way for Rya, but then let whip backwards to take Thomas full in the face. Thomas gritted his teeth in irritation, not realizing that his worries disappeared as his anger increased, much as Rynlin intended. Soon the trail leveled off and the trees thinned out. Thomas followed after his grandparents doggedly, staring daggers at Rynlin's back. Some of those branches had connected, and because of the cold the sting hurt all the more. After about a half-hour they reached the summit of Athala's Forge, the tallest mountain in the Kingdoms. The Circle stood before him on a plateau that stretched on into the distance.

The huge stone columns dominated everything around them. Most were two or three times the size of a normal man, each one several feet thick and only allowing for a short space between them. Once, their sides had displayed a sharp edge, but time, wind and the elements had worked against them, until their sharp sides became smooth. Strangely, the tops of the columns appeared untouched, retaining their original form — a pyramid several feet tall, a unicorn's horn carved into each face.

Thomas swept his gaze over the monoliths, captured by their stark beauty. The columns served as the outer boundary of the Circle, and in the very center of the stone giants stood an even larger stone, rising well above the other columns and reaching toward the sky like a beacon. It, too, had lost its sharp edges. Small steps, pitted and scarred by the elements but still intact, ran up one side to the flattened top.

Rynlin and Rya made their way toward the Circle as Thomas took in the structure. There were so many questions Thomas wanted to ask, yet both had serious expressions on their faces that did not invite conversation. The closer they got to the Circle, the more nervous Thomas became. As the first stone loomed up in front of them, Rynlin and Rya stopped. Rya gave him a quick hug before hurrying through the space between two columns. Rynlin nodded then stepped through as well. The time finally had arrived. At the end of the day he would know if he was meant to join the ranks of the Sylvana, and perhaps something more of his future than he really wanted to know.

Taking a deep breath to calm the butterflies that congregated in his stomach, Thomas walked between the two stones and stopped. Only a Sylvan Warrior could enter without an invitation, so he waited. To keep his legs from shaking because of his nervousness, he examined his surroundings. The Circle wasn't very large at all, it just seemed that way because of the monstrous stones that served as its boundary. Several dozen people deep in discussion stood in small groups. They had not yet noticed him. Rynlin and Rya ignored the others and walked across the Circle, going past the huge stone in the center and then standing in front of two columns.

Thomas studied some of the faces. Many appeared familiar thanks to Rynlin and Rya's lesson from the night before. Daran Sharban was the Sylvan Warrior who lived at the edge of the Highlands where it touched the Breaker. It was hard to misplace the curly red hair and beard and twinkling eyes. Rynlin always said that even though Daran was several hundred years old, the boy had never left him when he had become a man. Most of the Sylvan Warriors wore somber expressions; Daran an easy smile.

Some of the others he guessed at. A short, bald man with a few wisps of white hair falling victim to the strong breeze rushing across the plateau must be Tiro of Dunmoor. He stood at the base of the large column in the center of the Circle, known as the Stone. Thomas ran his eyes over the other Sylvan Warriors. The short man with the long, white beard that ran halfway down his chest must be Gavin of Ferranagh. He lived right next to the Western Ocean and was speaking with Teresa Nasoul. She called the Western Isle home. Thomas recognized her because of her silky white hair. Remarkably, she looked no older than he.

Talking with them was Brinn Kavolin, an extremely tall, slender man. He had a sharp, angular face and dark brown hair that continually fell into his eyes. Standing not too far away were the twins — Elisia and Aurelia Valeran from Kashel. He couldn't even begin to guess which was which. Off to the side stood the fiercest-looking person Thomas had ever laid eyes on. He had to be Catal Huyuk. Thomas had listened to Rynlin's stories about the man with some skepticism, thinking that his grandfather had embellished, as was his wont. Now he wondered if his grandfather had actually downplayed this hulking giant's achievements.

As Rynlin and Rya took up their positions across the Circle, the other Sylvan Warriors finally noticed him standing there. The Sylvana slowly scattered, each moving to stand in front of a different column. Many columns were empty. The Sylvana had never been a large group, and sadly now less than a hundred remained.

Tiro watched the activity around him with a cool eye, waiting patiently for each Warrior to find a place. He then walked slowly around the huge Stone, making sure that each Sylvan Warrior was ready. Satisfied, he climbed the steps of the Stone, careful of where he placed his feet. When he reached the top, he took a few moments to settle his white robe around him until it was exactly the way he wanted it.

"One asks entry into the Circle," bellowed Tiro in a voice louder than Thomas expected, his somber tone echoing across the plateau. "May he enter?"

"He may," answered the Sylvan Warriors, their eyes centered on the Stone, their voices solemn. Tiro beckoned to Thomas, motioning for him to approach.

Thomas breathed deeply to calm the butterflies that had multiplied in his stomach, then stepped forward. He walked slowly into the Circle, his eyes fixed on the Stone. He could feel the eyes of the Sylvana on him, studying him, already judging him. Thomas tried to appear calm and confident, his face a mask hiding the turmoil of his spirit. Did he really belong here? Thomas struggled with his doubts. Rynlin had told him every day for the past week that many had been summoned to face the challenges, and many had returned home in failure. When he reached the base of the Stone, he placed each foot carefully on the crumbling and brittle steps. Concentrating on not falling off the Stone took away some of his worry.

As he reached the smooth surface of the top, he looked across at the large, red face of Tiro. He wore the same expression as the other Sylvana — serious, even forbidding. By the set of Tiro's face, the rather rotund man took pleasure in his current, temporary position. He liked being the center of attention. Thomas had a feeling that Tiro would do what he could to draw out whatever was supposed to happen next, relishing every second atop the Stone. As if to confirm Thomas' suspicions, Tiro waited a few moments longer before beginning.

"For thousands of years the Sylvana have protected the Kingdoms," said Tiro, his voice carrying out over the plateau. "We are the defenders of nature, the power that gives life to the world. Once we were many; now we are few. Still, those who remain continue to uphold the responsibility that is ours, and ours alone."

Thomas briefly looked down from the Stone, taking in the solemn faces all around him. There was a sadness in their eyes as they remembered those who had died fighting against the Shadow Lord; many times fighting when no one else could, or would.

"Long ago, we joined with the Kingdoms, but no more. The kings and queens have forgotten what allows them to rule, what allows them to live. They have forgotten that their main purpose is to protect the land, the rivers, the people from the darkness that has threatened to blanket the world for millennia. The Kingdoms have forgotten, enveloped by the petty squabbles of weak men and women. But the Sylvana watch, and wait, for the time when we will ride forth once again to battle the Shadow Lord, and to protect nature from his minions."

Tiro paused dramatically, letting his words drift on the

wind. He then turned his intelligent eyes on Thomas. "You have been called to us, Thomas Keldragan Kestrel. We will see if you belong here in the Circle. Your skill with weapons is of little importance at the moment, though that will change. Besides, many of us don't need steel to fight." Tiro bit off the last word as if it were a piece of meat that had gone bad weeks before, his mouth twisting in disgust. His tone suggested that fighting with steel was barbaric and beneath him. His disapproving glance at the sword strapped onto Thomas' back confirmed it. "Instead, we test your inner strength and your knowledge of nature. The Shadow Lord has many weapons, and his evil is strong. Only the stoutest of heart and mind can survive." Tiro again paused for the greatest effect, letting Thomas absorb his words. "Are you ready for the first challenge?"

Thomas swallowed, his mouth having gone dry because of his nerves. It was time. Would he succeed? He scanned the Sylvana standing silent below him and found his grandparents. They, too, wore somber expressions on their faces, yet Rynlin locked eyes with him for an instant and nodded. Thomas smiled. His grandfather thought he was ready for what lay ahead. They had told him the night before that he could over-come the challenges. He just had to remember to take the time to think. Thankful for the show of support, Thomas stood up straight and looked Tiro squarely in the eyes.

"I am," he answered in a strong voice. Finally the wait was over. Whatever the outcome, he could put his worries to rest and find out what the next step in his life would bring.

8

UNFORTUNATE MEETING

"Good," said Tiro. "First, we will test your knowledge of the forest. Remove your weapons."

Thomas unbuckled his sword scabbard and lay the blade on the Stone. He then pulled the dagger at his hip from its sheath as well as one hidden in each of his boots, and two more from under the sleeves of his shirt, and placed them to the side. He felt naked without his weapons. While bending down he briefly met the gaze of Catal Huyuk and saw the big warrior smile for an instant. The dark and intimidating man obviously approved of Thomas' affinity for steel. At the same time, a look of disappointment flashed across Tiro's face, but Thomas ignored him.

"Return to the Circle in three hours' time. The use of the Talent is forbidden. If you do not return in three hours, you fail."

Return to the Circle? What did he mean by— a brilliant white light flashed directly in front of Thomas, forcing him to duck away. He was careful not to shift his feet, though. He didn't want to fall off the Stone, as there was barely enough room for two people to stand on it. Black spots danced in front of his eyes and the seconds dragged into minutes before his vision cleared. When he rose to his feet again, the haze gone from his eyes, his mouth opened in shock. He was no longer on the Stone. In fact, he had absolutely no idea where he was.

"The first surprise of the day," Thomas muttered to himself. He didn't think it would be the last either.

Only a few seconds before he had stood on top of the highest peak in the Highlands. Now, he was stuck in the middle of the densest forest he had ever encountered. The Burren, with its grasping vines and prickly bushes, didn't compare to his current predicament. Heart trees rose several hundred feet into the sky all around him, the massive trunks and craggy roughness of the bark reminding him of the Isle of Mist. The bushes that surrounded him were twice his height and so thick and tangled they were a more effective barrier than any stonewall could ever be. The bushes pushed in all around him, leaving him little room to maneuver. This wasn't a forest, it was a prison. Worst of all, the dense canopy prevented any light from getting through, creating an unnatural darkness. Though it was early morning, it appeared to be night.

There was no place to go. He didn't know where he was in relation to the Circle, and even if he did, trying to get there from here could take days. Making his way through the dense overgrowth would be virtually impossible. The thought of using the Talent crossed his mind, however briefly, but he recalled Tiro's words. The Sylvana would know, and he would fail.

No matter. First, he needed to determine his exact position in relation to the Circle. Then he could move on to the next step. Thomas glanced around quickly. Even with his sharp vision, he failed to pierce the green veil spread across his eyes by the surrounding vegetation. That left him with no other choice.

Digging his fingers into the bark of the nearest heart tree, Thomas began pulling himself up. Although the bark scratched and tore at his palms, it offered excellent foot- and handholds. He went as fast as he could, finding crevices and tiny gaps to aid his climb. He ignored the droplets of sweat dripping down his forehead and into his eyes because of the strain of the climb. Despite the cool temperatures, Thomas silently thanked Rynlin for suggesting he leave his cloak behind and wear only a loose shirt and breeks. He continued his ascent, remembering not to look down. Heights didn't bother him, but looking down at the forest floor could disorient him, and that was something he wanted to avoid.

The next time Rynlin or Rya mention a challenge, he told himself, *I'm going to make sure they give me a better explanation. No more secrets.* He promised himself that he would follow through on that pledge, though he knew his grandparents would remain as recalcitrant as ever.

Finally, after climbing more than a hundred feet up the trunk, Thomas grabbed the first branch. Setting his foot on it, he pulled himself up. The branches of the heart tree functioned much like a ladder and made the going easier. Yet, though he had climbed halfway up the tree, he still couldn't see through the branches. He'd have to go higher, where the foliage thinned out. Grabbing the branch above him, Thomas continued his ascent, this time with a greater sense of urgency. Twenty minutes had passed. Time was disappearing quickly.

After another short climb, Thomas found what he was looking for — a break through the branches. He had almost reached the top. The tree swayed gently from side to side in rhythm to the wind, increasing the danger. Hooking his arm around a thick, sturdy branch for safety, Thomas gazed out across the forest. It stretched for several leagues from his current vantage point, with no mountain in sight. He moved cautiously over to the other side of the tree, again securing his arm around a branch. The leaves were denser here, so Thomas swept them from his line of sight with his free hand.

As he reached out to pull a few more branches out of his way, a strong gust of wind buffeted the tree. Caught out of position, Thomas grasped wildly for something to hold onto as his hand slipped from the branch and his feet went out from under him. Digging his fingers into the bark of the branch where his feet had been, he held on desperately as the tree swayed violently in the wind.

Just as fast as the gust of wind struck, it subsided. Thomas sighed with relief. He looked below him, unsure of how he succeeded in grabbing the branch. The branches that blocked his view of the ground surely would have broken his fall, in addition to most of the bones in his body. Luck. That was the only way to explain it. Otherwise, he'd be down there right now, a victim of the ultimate failure.

"Nothing is ever easy," he murmured as he pulled himself back onto the branch. He again grabbed hold of the limb with one hand, careful to make sure he had a good grip before peeking through the branches. One almost fatal mistake for the day was more than enough.

There! He could see it. The peaks of the Highlands were off in the distance, and Athala's Forge rose right in front of him. Thankfully, he was not at its very base. Instead, the forest that surrounded him ran along the upper slopes of these mountains. He must be on some sort of plateau. That still didn't help him, though. With almost an hour gone, he stood no closer to his goal. Only two hours left. Two hours, and he still had a league or more of forest to traverse, to say nothing of the climb of several thousand feet that waited for him after that.

Thomas squeezed his free hand into a fist in frustration. He didn't have enough time. How was he supposed to get to the Circle in two hours? It would take him days just to make his way through the undergrowth. It just wasn't fair! Thomas immediately clamped down on the emotions that threatened to break through to the surface. His anger would not help him now. He needed to think. He had to find a way. If others had passed this test, so could he.

Wait a second! The answer was right in front of him. Or rather below him. He could use the trees as his road. About a hundred feet below him, the branches of many of the trees collided with one another, and they were so thick they could easily hold his weight. He could use the branches as a path as he did when he helped that girl in the Burren. Princess, he should say. She certainly was beautiful. Very beautiful, as a matter of fact, especially with those blue eyes of hers and raven-black hair. Thomas dismissed the image that had formed in his mind. No time for that now.

Thomas descended from his vantage point until he found a branch that looked about right. As he stepped onto it, he took a moment to clear his mind. Using the Talent was forbidden, but Tiro had not said anything about nature. During his lessons Thomas had learned that concentrating as he did when controlling the Talent could serve many other useful purposes. For example, it allowed him to get closer to nature, to feel and see the myriad activity around him, without having to draw on the power of nature. Rya explained that though it was similar to using the Talent, you were not actually taking hold of it. It simply resulted from his being closer to nature than most other people. Anyone could do it, in fact, if the person knew how. But only a few did. That's why he could smell the sea from leagues away or taste the wind or feel the warmth of the sun on a cloudy day, when others couldn't.

Concentrating as he did when using the Talent, Thomas began walking across the branch. This deep in the tree, he didn't have to worry about the wind, he only had to focus on where he placed his feet. Soon, he stepped across to another branch, with no more than a finger's breadth separating the two. Thomas picked up his pace to a fast walk. His mind closed out everything around him except for the branches he traveled across. He didn't even look down to know where to place his feet. He could sense the branch underneath his feet, feel the texture of it.

Thomas reached the next tree and jumped across a slight gap, landing solidly on the next branch that formed his unique pathway. As his concentration grew stronger, he sensed the sap running through the tree's limbs. He could taste it, smell it. He felt as if he were actually a part of the tree. Gradually, he picked up his pace even more; first to a trot, then to a run. A particular memory jumped into his mind of when he raced through the forest on the Isle of Mist with his friend Beluil, reveling in the excitement of the competition.

Branch after branch passed beneath his feet in a blur as he continued on his course. In a few places, Thomas jumped down to a lower branch or climbed up to a new one, but it didn't slow him. He moved by instinct, letting his feet pick the best path. For a time, he even closed his eyes. The limb he ran across appeared in his mind. He could make out the texture of the bark where a woodpecker had looked for a meal and a bolt of lightning had charred a branch three hundred years before. It was a remarkable experience, and one to savor. He had never felt so close to nature before. He had never felt so much at ease. He just might make it. He just might.

Thomas stopped abruptly. He had concentrated so much on where he was going that he failed to pay attention to his surroundings. He judged that he was close to the end of the forest, yet the darkness was now complete. The sun should have brightened the gloom at least a bit. A cold wind brushed against him, chilling him to the bone.

Strangely, the branches themselves remained still despite

the gust. Even more ominous, the forest was silent. Thomas strained his senses, searching for some clue to explain the change. Yet, he picked out nothing unusual except a vague feeling of uneasiness. He crinkled his nose in distaste. A strange odor swept over him, one of decay and death. Something was wrong, terribly wrong.

A prickling sensation along Thomas' spine alerted him that he was not alone. Jumping around, he almost fell off the branch. He shuffled back a few steps. A beautiful woman stood before him, her hand extended to where his shoulder had been just a second before. The long, dark chestnut hair made him think of his—

"You're right, Thomas," said the figure before him. "You're right, though we have never met. You know me in your heart. I am Marya, your mother."

Thomas flinched involuntarily. His mother? But how could it be? Ever since he was a child he had dreamed of what it would be like to meet her face to face, but it was impossible. She died during his birth.

"How could you be here?" he asked in a shaky voice. Dozens of emotions whirled through his mind, drowning out the tiny voice of reason, a voice screaming at him that he was in danger.

"I am strong in the Talent, as are you, Thomas." Marya stepped closer, until she could almost touch him. The odor of death grew stronger. She stopped when it appeared that Thomas was going to step back away from her. "There are many things I can do. Talyn told you that I had died, but he lied. He wanted to keep you from me. For years I have searched for you. And now I have finally found you."

Thomas frowned. Talyn died saving him from the reivers and Ogren. It couldn't be as she said. His grandfather had been a man of honor. Yet his mother stood before him. "But why?"

"He was like the others at the Crag, Thomas. He was afraid

of me, and what I could do with the Talent. He thought that if he kept me away from you, you could escape my family's legacy."

"But—"

It was almost too much for him to absorb. Was his mother speaking the truth? Everyone at the Crag had been afraid of him. That was certainly true. Had his grandfather been as well? Thomas stepped back quickly, heeding the small voice that struggled to break free from his swirling emotions. Marya had moved closer to him. There was something about her that felt wrong. The image of an open crypt popped into his mind.

Marya reached out her hand. "Come with me, Thomas. Come with me now. There is so much we need to learn about each other. So much that we have missed." At first, Marya's voice was soft and sweet. It turned harsher and more demanding when he hesitated. "Come with me, Thomas! Come with me!"

Thomas looked at the figure of his mother, his feet rooted to the branch as he took in everything about her. She appeared just as he had dreamed of her. Then he noticed her eyes. In his dreams, they were green, playful and full of life. Now they were black and lifeless, filled with the cold of the grave. Marya inched closer to him again. Thomas stepped back in response.

"No, I can't. I must—"

"Come with me, Thomas! Come with me now!" Marya shrieked. Thomas danced back from her. The tiny voice in his mind finally broke its chain, screaming at him to run, to get away. This couldn't be happening. Talyn would never lie to him. His mother was dead.

The figure before him, sensing his fear, charged forward. Thomas dodged out of the way, almost falling from the branch. Luckily, he maintained his balance. The creature that was Marya screeched in anger at missing its prey and turned back toward him. Thomas watched in horror as Marya's hands changed into twisted claws, her face becoming a mask of hatred, the skin tightening around her skull and her eyes burning a bright red. A ghoul stood before him now.

The voice in his mind told him to stay away, and he knew with certainty that one touch from the ghoul would mean his death. But now this creature blocked his path. The ghoul lunged for him, hungry for a warm soul. With nowhere else to go, Thomas jumped down from his perch, falling twenty feet through the air to the branch below him. His feet slipped off the bark as he landed awkwardly, but he caught the limb with his hands, ignoring the pain that shot through his palms as the rough bark bit into his flesh. He quickly pulled himself onto the branch and saw the ghoul looking down at him evilly, not yet willing to end the pursuit.

Giving in to his instincts, Thomas ran across the branch in a burst of speed, hoping to escape the creature. He tried to regain his concentration, but his fear prevented it. He sensed the ghoul as it followed along above him, easily tracking his movements. For several minutes he ran from tree to tree, his terror driving him forward. When would the forest end? The ghoul kept up with him easily. When?

A bolt of fear shot through him as he heard a thud behind him. The creature had jumped down onto his branch. The ghoul screeched in triumph, confident of its victory, knowing it was almost time to feed. Not daring to look back, Thomas ran across the branches, the tiny voice in his mind screaming in terror. He felt the ghoul reaching for him, and he imagined the dead hand closing around his shoulder, draining the life from his body. Ignoring his fear, Thomas focused on the branches before him. The unnatural darkness was growing lighter. He was almost there. Almost—

Sensing the ghoul was gaining, now only a few fingers away,

Thomas jumped down from the branch, landing heavily on the one below. The ghoul howled in anger, having come so close to its prize and then losing its chance. Thomas didn't wait to see what it would do. He had reached the edge of the forest.

Jumping down onto the limb of one of the trees that nestled up against the mountains, he started the difficult climb down. He ignored the cuts and scrapes on his hands as he used the branches as a ladder, his fear threatening to choke him. The ghoul followed him down the tree, and it was gaining as its claws tore into the rough bark. Its raspy breath sounded like a death knell in Thomas' ears. After reaching the lowest limb, he still had more than a hundred feet to go before his feet touched the ground. Feeling the urgency of his situation, he hurried down the tree trunk as fast as he could, finding crevices in the bark for his hands and feet, but this time sliding more than climbing, his fear of the ghoul stronger than his fear of falling.

Two times he almost lost his grip because of his quest for speed, but he didn't care. The ghoul was almost upon him. The musty odor of the grave played through his nostrils, urging him downward. Suddenly, Thomas' feet hit the earth. Not bothering to look up, he ran through the brush in a burst of speed, fighting off the vines and branches that sought to delay him. And then he was free, the darkness giving way to light, the forest to a flat plain. The ghoul howled in anger, stopping at the tree line and not daring to enter the sunlight.

"Finally," he whispered to himself. His body shuddered at the memory of what had just occurred. Yet, as he looked back at the forest, the shadowy darkness had retreated, and with it the hungering ghoul that pursued him.

Taking a few moments to catch his breath, Thomas gazed up at his final hurdle, the time he had lost in the forest weighing him down. If he was right, the Circle sat atop the cliff, which just happened to rise several thousand feet into the air. Normally such a climb wouldn't be a problem, but with such a steep incline, and a surface composed of loose shale with several large boulders tipped precariously on their edges, it would be difficult at best.

He'd have to avoid those boulders at all costs. The way things were going today they'd probably start rolling down the slope at the slightest movement. If he wasn't careful and slipped, a fall from a heart tree would be pleasant compared to sliding down this rocky slope with a few large rocks following after him.

Half an hour left, maybe less, he judged. No time to waste. Thomas started his climb, digging into the loose scrabble as best he could and hoping that a ghoul or some other hideous creature didn't wait for him at the top. Because of the slope, a trot was as good a pace as he could achieve. To maintain his balance, he hunched over at the waist and leaned forward.

Many times he used his hands to help pull himself up the cliff as large pieces of shale gave way beneath his feet and he slid dangerously back down the slope. Only his frantic attempts to dig his hands into the cliff face kept him from tumbling head over heels back down to the plain. Though unavoidable, his efforts irritated the cuts and scrapes plaguing his hands, which he ignored.

Each time the shale gave way, he redoubled his efforts, pulling and lunging his way upward, ignoring the pinpricks of pain that ran down his arms every time he forced his hands into the loose rock. He was halfway up the slope with only fifteen minutes left. He had to go faster, but how? For every two steps he took in the loose rock, he slid back one. Giving way to caution, Thomas pushed himself forward, moving as fast as he could up the slope. If he stepped on another large piece of shale at his current speed, he didn't think he'd catch himself in time before he started falling backward. He didn't care. He was almost to the top. How much time remained?

Eyes focused on the shifting surface beneath his feet, his

mind centered strictly on his task, it took him a second to realize that the ground had begun to shake. The soft rumbling sound grew louder, and it was coming toward him. Looking up in shock, Thomas leaped to his right, landing heavily on his side and sliding several feet back down the slope as a large rock rolled past him. In the beginning he had done his best to avoid them, but now, in the interest of speed, he had forgotten about the boulders. Thomas cursed in frustration. The edge of the cliff was no more than two hundred feet away. He was almost there, and he had ten minutes left. Ten minutes! He could still make—

A boulder cascaded toward him, larger than any of the others. It had been lying right on the lip of the cliff face, and now it rolled directly toward him, hopping and skipping its way down the slope. It was massive, blotting out the sun and putting Thomas in darkness. The analytical part of Thomas' mind guessed that it weighed several tons. The practical part told him to run, but he had nowhere to go. It was coming too fast for him to move out of its way.

The rock beneath Thomas' feet gave way, forcing him to drop to one knee to retain his balance. Wait a second. His sliding body had created a deep gash in the loose rock of the cliff face. Several of the shale pieces that had broken apart were almost as large as he was. Maybe it would work. Just maybe. He really didn't have a choice, nor the time.

Diving into the hole he had made, Thomas quickly pulled a large piece of shale over the top, covering the hole. He then used his legs to support the makeshift ceiling of his burrow. The large boulder gained speed rapidly as it rolled down the hillside, leaving a deep wake behind it, much like a ship cutting through the sea with its prow, and sweeping the loose rock and shale before it. The first small rock hit Thomas' structure and harmlessly bounced off it. Then another followed, and another, each bigger than the last. It was working. The boulders were rolling right over him. Now for the real test. The massive boulder was almost upon him.

A detached part of him wondered at the improbability of the whole thing. How one moment he had almost reached the top, and now, in just a few seconds, he waited for a boulder to flatten him into the cliff. The ground shook even more, and because of it, Thomas' body slid backwards down the slope. As a result, he lost control of the piece of shale he used as a shield. Thomas dug his fingers into the hillside, desperately grasping several large rocks sticking out of the soil. Suddenly, the dim shadow of the sky disappeared, replaced by black. Holding his breath, Thomas braced himself for the collision. As the boulder hit the piece of shale, the tremendous weight pushed Thomas' legs down into his chest. He tried to breathe, but couldn't. Every muscle in his body felt like it was about to explode.

In an instant, the pressure dissipated. Thomas gulped down a breath of air, grateful that the piece of shale had not cracked under the weight of the boulder. It had worked. It had actually worked!

"Thank you," he whispered to the piece of shale as he gently placed it on the hillside. Getting unsteadily to his feet, Thomas wiped his sweaty, bloody palms onto his breeks. The top was only a few hundred feet away, and the large boulder had cleared the loose rock out of his way. Leaning toward the cliff face with his body, Thomas ran up the newly created path. Only a few minutes remained.

Finally reaching the top of the cliff, relief swept through him. The Circle was right in front of him. Ignoring the pain in his hands and the stiffness in his legs, Thomas ran toward the huge columns. With a final burst of speed, he leapt into the Circle and ascended the Stone as quickly as he dared. The Sylvan Warriors remained where they were when he had first disappeared, standing stoically in front of a particular column. They watched him with hard eyes as he climbed the final steps of the Stone. Even Rynlin and Rya had a look of indifference on their faces. Had he failed? He couldn't have. Could he? A knot of fear rose in his throat. Standing again in front of Tiro, Thomas prepared himself for the worst.

9

THE VILLAGE

"It was very clever of you to walk the trees," he said in a loud voice so all could hear. "Most struggle through the forest on the ground and become hopelessly lost."

Thomas looked at Tiro in concern. Had he passed? That's all he wanted to know. Tiro saw it on Thomas' face and smiled, enjoying the suspense.

"You have overcome the first challenge. You know the forest and the dangers that lurk there; you are a part of it." Thomas let out a sigh of relief that was short-lived. "On to the second challenge. This is a test of your inner strength. Three dreams await you."

Stands on high. The words echoed through his mind. His daydreaming would have to wait. He should be giving his full attention to Tiro and his next challenge. *Stands on high.* Rynlin had explained his theory regarding the prophecy, and now he was here.

He glanced around the Stone. The Sylvana stared back at him. At first, he had taken their expressions to be ones of indifference. That remained somewhat, but had something else worked its way in as well? Hope, maybe. Could it be hope?

Stands on high. Maybe it was. Maybe Rynlin had explained his theory to them as well, or some of the Sylvana had developed their own theories. *Stands on high.* Now was not the time to think on it. There was too much at stake.

"In each dream you must do what is right, and that is something for you to decide. But I warn you, the choice is not always easily made. There is no absolute right or absolute wrong, despite what you might think. There is only individual judgment. Let your judgment be your guide. If you choose wrongly, you will fail, and you may die. Therefore, think before you act. Are you ready?"

Die? A shiver ran up Thomas' spine, remembering the ghoul and how close its cold, deadly touch had come. Rynlin and Rya had conveniently forgotten to tell him about that possibility. They had simply said that if he failed, he could never join the Sylvana. He'd have to talk to them about their slip when this was over. If he survived, of course.

Thomas nodded. The bright white light greeted him once more, again blinding him for a moment. When the spots cleared from his eyes, he found himself in a large field just beyond the outer boundary of a small village. Thomas turned in a circle to get his bearings. He was completely and thoroughly lost. The mountains of the Highlands were nowhere in sight. A few stalks of corn still remained, crushed beneath the feet of the workers, who had just harvested the field.

The village itself was unremarkable, with a small road running through its center passing by wooden cottages with thatched roofs. Most farmers couldn't afford stone. A small green formed the center of the village. The villagers probably gathered there for their holidays and meetings. Thomas was thoroughly confused now. Why had Tiro sent him here? Judging from the position of the sun, much of the morning still remained, so most of the farmers would be out tending their crops.

Seeing nothing of interest in the surrounding forest, Thomas walked toward the village. He stopped in his tracks. A quiver of arrows was at his hip with a bow across his back. Thomas slipped it over his head. It was his bow and his arrows. But how did they get here? He hadn't brought them with him. No weapons were allowed for the first challenge. Of course, Tiro had said nothing about weapons this time.

Shrugging it off, Thomas entered the village with bow in hand. Smoke drifted into the sky from the cottage chimneys, carrying with it the wonderful smell of baking bread. Across the green several women sat together talking, a few quite animatedly. He wondered about what. At first he thought it might be because of him. A stranger walking into a small town could set off quite a ruckus. But, no, it couldn't be him. They hadn't seen him yet. Some of the women gestured, but in a different direction.

Thomas walked halfway to the green when the rumble of horses' hooves shattered the quiet. The women who sat together so placidly just an instant before now ran in fright. Why would they—

Ten horsemen, their long hair tied back in braids, galloped into the village. Wearing black leather armor, they held whips and lassoes. Slavers! The lead rider singled out a young woman and charged forward. She screamed in terror as the horse bore down on her. Before he knew what he was doing, Thomas ran toward the chaos. The rider was no more than a few paces behind the fleeing girl when he lashed out with his whip. The hard leather bit into the woman's arm, opening a long cut. She fell to the ground in pain, the whip still entangled about her arm.

All across the green similar scenes played out. Another slaver had already caught a young girl, probably no more than twelve years old. One horseman had missed on his first pass, but was now coming around for a second, gleefully pursuing a young woman with auburn hair. For the slavers their work had become a game, as they realized that no one could challenge them.

The first rider jumped down from his horse and swaggered toward the girl, who sat on the ground in a daze. She stared in disbelief at the cut on her arm, no longer understanding what was going on around her. The man reached down and took hold of her other arm, giving the girl a leer.

The situation soon became frighteningly clear to the young woman. She frantically tried to pull her arm free, but she couldn't break the slaver's hold. Tears ran down her face as her fear and desperation grew. Suddenly, she fell backward in the grass, free of the rider's grasp. The man still stood above her, but with a glazed look in his eyes. A second later, he toppled over, a long arrow sticking out from the center of his back.

Thomas had acted without thinking, but he didn't care. Once again, he didn't have time to think. It always happened that way. He just acted according to his instinct. Certain that his first arrow struck true, Thomas pulled another from his quiver. He had sprinted to the center of the green, and now stood there with his legs spread apart, one slightly in front of the other. Nocking another arrow to his bow, he drew back on the cord. Sighting on the rider who had already captured a woman, he released.

The second attacker fell dead with an arrow through the eye. Both were large men, much like their comrades, and displayed the quick sure movements of soldiers. They were accustomed to battle, as it was an almost daily part of their lives. Nevertheless, a single bolt with a steel tip had an amazing capacity to level the playing field.

Thomas quickly moved on to the next slaver, and then the next. In seconds, five men were dead. The other raiders finally noticed that someone was actually fighting back, initially thinking that the men of the village had returned from the fields. Much to their surprise they saw a single boy standing boldly in the middle of the green.

Three immediately charged forward, kicking their horses to a gallop. The urge to run briefly rose within him, but Thomas beat it down. He stood his ground and calmly placed another arrow onto his bow. Shooting at a moving target was much more difficult, and with three charging toward him, he couldn't afford to make a mistake. Thomas waited just a moment longer, then raised his bow, sighted and released in one smooth motion. A second arrow immediately followed the first, and a third the second.

The three slavers never knew what hit them, falling dead to the green, pierced by Thomas' yard-long arrows. Their panic-stricken horses continued down the road. The two raiders who remained at the far edge of the green stared in shock at their friends lying face down in the short grass. They considered themselves brave men, but if this boy could so easily dispatch three men on horseback, how difficult would it be for him if there were only two? They wisely decided that the time for valor had passed.

Turning their horses back the way they had come, the two slavers tried to escape the village. Unfortunately for them, Thomas was not in a forgiving mood. They made it as far as the last house on the village's outskirts before steel-tip arrows knocked them from their saddles.

It was over. The village was safe and none of the women seemed to be hurt badly. He regretted the killing, to a degree. The fact that he had killed ten men in a matter of minutes hit him squarely in the gut, the gorge rising in his throat. He fought the urge to empty his stomach, trying to ignore the bad taste in his mouth. He didn't enjoy killing these men, and he wasn't proud of what he had done, but it proved necessary in this situation.

He thought his grandfather, Talyn, would approve of his

judgment. The sick feeling subsided and he began walking toward the women to see if he could help those injured by the attackers when a bright, white light flashed before him. Once again, black spots danced before his eyes. Thomas sighed in frustration. This was becoming wearisome.

When Thomas opened his eyes, he stood atop the stone with Tiro. The Sylvana remained as still as the stone monoliths towering above them: quiet, forbidding, dispassionate. Yet Thomas was certain he felt something percolating within them. He was sure of it. Hope. He could see it in their eyes now, even if their faces continued to hide it.

Then another thought struck him. He should have realized it before, but he had been so busy thinking of what he had to do, he had failed to pay attention to what was going on around him. He had sensed the energy from the beginning. The Sylvana, at least those who could control the Talent, were using the Circle as a focal point to combine their strength and bring Thomas back and forth from wherever they sent him or create the scenario he had to respond to, and watch what he did most likely. It was an interesting discovery on his part, but one he couldn't explore at the moment.

10

CHOICES

"The Sylvana are warriors, people of action," intoned Tiro. "You made the correct choice. On to the second dream." In another flash of white light, Thomas left the Circle. This time, though, he closed his eyes before the white light blinded him. When he opened his eyes, his vision was clear.

Or was it? He stood in the middle of the most lavish, luxurious room he had ever seen. It was enormous. The ceiling rose twenty feet into the air, and upon the lacquered wood an artist had painted various scenes. One showed a castle sitting majestically in the middle of a bay, a long causeway connecting it to the mainland. The Rock of Ballinasloe, Thomas assumed. No other fortress resembled it. Another depicted a man standing on a hill, his golden armor shining brightly in the sunlight. Ollav Fola perhaps. The others Thomas didn't bother to examine.

Dozens of windows rose from floor to ceiling, showering the room with bits of green, blue and red as the sun shone through the beautiful stained glass. Even the furniture was magnificent, and Thomas usually didn't pay attention to such things. A stool was a stool and a table a table. Though there were only a few tables and chairs lining the walls, leaving the center of the room bare, they were all intricately carved with swirls, points and curls. The back of one chair illustrated a dolphin leaping out of the water, another an eagle gliding through the sky. He had never seen such sophisticated and precise craftsmanship before.

Thomas examined a table more closely. To his surprise his feet sank into the floor as he walked around the piece of furniture. A dark blue carpet lay beneath his feet, which were barely visible because of its thickness. It was then that he noticed his clothes. He wore a white silk shirt, a pair of blue trousers with gold running up the sides and soft leather boots that came to just above his ankle. A red sash ran around his waist, and a gold chain at his hip held a dagger.

Thomas pulled it out of its sheath. Truly remarkable. The blue steel joined to an ivory hilt encrusted with diamonds, opals and moonstones. Thomas quickly returned the dagger to its sheath. He had never held something so valuable in his hands, and it made him uncomfortable. He was not used to such wealth. It didn't feel right. Nothing about the room felt right, in fact. He didn't belong here.

As he stood there pondering what to do next, his forehead crinkled in thought, the door on the far side opened silently. A beautiful young woman stepped into the room. Thomas' frown turned into a look of surprise. It was her. The girl from the Burren. She wore a dark blue dress with white lace at the collar and sleeve. Her long, raven black hair curled around her face. His heart missed a beat when he saw her smile. She was the most beautiful woman he had ever seen.

What was her name? He should have remembered it. He had heard it at the glade. What was it? Kaylie. That's right. Kaylie. And she was coming toward him. Thomas gulped, trying to swallow his nerves. As she drew closer, his heart melted. The dress complemented her sea-blue eyes perfectly. Thomas smiled, attempting to mask his discomfort.

Her smile grew wider and her eyes danced with delight in response. He couldn't take his eyes from her. If he spent the last of his days staring at her face, he would die a happy man. Wait a second. Kaylie wasn't stopping. She was only a few feet from him now, and her smile had become a mischievous grin. Not knowing what else to do, Thomas held his ground.

Finally Kaylie stopped, yet she was so close Thomas felt her breath on his neck. Slowly she reached upward, her soft hands taking hold of his cheeks and drawing his lips to hers. Thomas closed his eyes in delight. An unfamiliar yearning rose up within him. Thomas hugged her to him. This excited Kaylie even more, her kiss becoming more urgent, more demanding. He didn't have any idea what to make of his current situation, but he didn't care. The uneasiness he had originally experienced dissipated. After much too brief a time Kaylie pulled away from him, but not so far as to require Thomas to remove his arms from her waist.

"Patience, Thomas," said Kaylie, a sly grin on her face. "Tomorrow we will be able to do this whenever we want rather than having to sneak a kiss in private." Her voice was soft, but commanding. She was used to giving orders. To his ears, though, it sounded like music.

"Tomorrow?" he asked in some confusion. Her eyes had captured him once again, and he surrendered meekly.

"Yes, silly," she said, tapping him lightly on the shoulder in mock anger. "Tomorrow. How could you forget?"

"Forget? I didn't forget." Thomas had absolutely no idea what Kaylie was talking about.

"I should hope not. Forgetting about our wedding tomorrow would certainly be the wrong way to begin our marriage."

Wedding? Thomas immediately closed his mouth once he realized he had opened it in shock. He was marrying Kaylie?

Now he was thoroughly confused. Thomas felt Kaylie's hands on his cheeks once more, and his worries disappeared as he kissed her again. He pulled her tightly against him once more, relishing the feel of her body against his.

The kiss grew more passionate, and more passionate still, when the sound of someone walking down the hallway outside the room traveled through the open door. Kaylie jumped back from Thomas in fright, hurriedly working out the tiny wrinkles that had formed where her dress had pressed up against him. Married to Kaylie? What was going on?

"I didn't come in here just so you could have some fun," she said sternly, though her eyes twinkled in delight. Women certainly did have a strange way about them. Some day Thomas would have to ask Rynlin about that. Then again, maybe he should talk to someone else. Rynlin's skill with women, as demonstrated with Rya, often left something to be desired. "I came here because my cousins have arrived, and I want you to meet them. Now come along, Thomas. We don't want to keep them waiting."

Stepping forward, Kaylie gave him a final, quick kiss on the lips before taking him by the hand and pulling him out into the hallway. With kisses like that, he could get used to this quite easily.

Thomas walked hand in hand with Kaylie as she led him down a long corridor lined with huge tapestries hanging from the wall. Sunlight illuminated the hallway through large, rectangular windows regularly spaced along its length.

"Now don't forget, Thomas," Kaylie began telling him. "My aunt's name is Matile. She's the one in black. Her husband died ten years ago, but she refuses to wear anything else. And my two cousins are Julee and Lorela. Julee's the tall one with black hair, Lorela's the short one with brown hair." Kaylie's words floated over Thomas as he watched this beautiful young lady out of the corner of his eye. Marry Kaylie? He couldn't believe his luck.

If you choose wrongly you will fail. What? Thomas shook his head in confusion. Was he hearing voices? Why would he have to choose?

Thomas noticed that Kaylie had slowed her pace. Two men walked toward them from the other end of the hall. He recognized the one on the left as Kaylie's father, Gregory. The other looked familiar. Thomas and Kaylie waited for the two to approach. Her hand gripped his tightly. She glanced at him in worry, the mischief gone from her eyes.

Something tickled at his memory. The man with Gregory reminded him of someone, but who? He was a Highlander, that was easy enough to figure out. He wore brown trousers, a green shirt and a dark green cloak that flapped along in his wake. The dust of the road covered the man, and he hadn't bothered to clean a small cut on his forehead, the dried blood having congealed in his slate grey hair just above his right eye. His face held a grim expression.

Coban? Could it be him? Thomas hadn't seen him in years, but it certainly did look like the Highland Swordmaster. It was him. He'd recognize that craggy face and hard eyes anywhere. What was he doing here? Kaylie's hand tightened even more over his own. Thomas smiled down at her reassuringly, then turned his attention back to the two men who stopped in front of them.

"Milord," said Coban, falling to his knee in front of Thomas. Thomas was taken aback by the action. What was going on? And why was Kaylie about to cry?

"Coban?" he asked hesitantly, still not completely sure.

"Yes, Thomas," said Gregory, his voice grim. "Coban arrived just moments ago. He demanded to see you at once. I thought it best to comply."

"Milord," began Coban. There was an intensity in his eyes,

brought on by desperation. "The Highlands are under attack. Ogren, Fearhounds and Shades have broken through our northern defenses. In a matter of days they'll reach the Crag. We need you, milord."

"You need me?" It was too much for him to comprehend. When he was growing up most of the people in the Crag wanted nothing to do with him. Now they wanted him back?

"We can't stop them," continued Coban. "Only you can. Only the Lost Kestrel can lead us to victory."

Tears streamed down Kaylie's face. Thomas tried to offer her some comfort, but she pulled away from him and buried her head in her father's shoulder instead. Gregory's expression turned sad. Thomas stood there, feeling more alone than ever before.

"And if I don't go back with you?" he asked Coban. Why should he return to the Highlands? His people hadn't cared about him while he was there.

"Then the Highlands will die, Thomas. Many of us have treated you poorly, but we are still your people. The Lost Kestrel must return."

The finality of Coban's words stung Thomas to his core. The Highlands would die. Yet if he returned to the Highlands, would he ever see Kaylie again? Why now? Why the day before his wedding? Why did he have to choose? Return to a people who didn't care about him until they needed him and break Kaylie's heart, or stay here and marry the most beautiful woman in the world? It should have been an easy choice. But it wasn't.

Torn on the inside, it felt as if two warriors had taken hold of his heart, each one tugging on it in an attempt to sway his decision. He could make the easy decision, and stay here with Kaylie. He had no doubt they would have a wonderful life together, and he would finally be free of his past, free of the problems and responsibilities. But then the Highlands would be no more. And it would be his fault. Could he place his own interests above those of his people?

Thomas closed his eyes for a moment, trying to think. *You must do what you must do. You must do what you must do.* The voice kept playing through his mind. It sounded like his grandmother's. Thomas realized he didn't really have much choice at all. Kaylie continued to sob into her father's shoulder, as if she already knew what he would do. Stepping forward, he kissed her lightly on the back of her head. It only increased her tears.

Nodding at Coban, he started walking down the hallway. Coban quickly caught up with him and the two made for the stables. Each step away from Kaylie made the tightness in his chest increase just a bit more, until finally he felt as if he couldn't breathe. Kaylie's cries echoed in his ears as he entered the stable yard. He felt as if his heart had shriveled up and died.

The blinding flash of white light beckoned. Thomas rubbed his eyes, trying to rid his vision of the spots dancing before him, which were now joined by two images of Tiro. One Tiro was quite enough in Thomas' opinion.

Tiro ignored the anger so obvious on Thomas' face. He had seen much the same thing many times before. Although the dreams always differed based on the individual, the choices to be made remained the same. In Tiro's opinion, how the challenges affected the person was immaterial. The only thing that mattered was that the candidate passed. He knew firsthand that life was not easy, and the choices offered in life were hard, especially for a Sylvan Warrior. But the choices had to be made nonetheless.

11

***

A PRELUDE

"The Sylvan Warriors are a people of honor," Tiro intoned. "Often we must choose between two competing responsibilities. Knowing which takes precedence, despite our dislike of the choice made, sets us apart from others. You have made the correct choice. On to the third dream. Though the restriction is now removed. You may use the Talent if required."

Wait. What? Thomas closed his eyes quickly, just barely avoiding the blinding flash of light he was expecting. Maybe he wasn't fast enough after all. The spots had not appeared, but he couldn't see anything at all. He stood in total darkness. Slowly, his eyes adjusted.

He stood in the center of an enormous chamber. Its ceiling, several hundred feet above the tiled floor, was made of a glass dome that allowed a few tiny rays of light to enter. It did little to dissipate the shadows, however. Thomas saw that he wore his own clothes this time, and his sword — his grandfather's sword — was strapped to his back. The hair on the back of his neck prickled, and the blood flowed more quickly through his veins. He had been given weapons at the green. If he now had his sword, he would probably have need of it. Tiro explained that you could die during the tests if you failed. The battle he had fought on the green had certainly been real enough.

Thomas remained in the center of the room for several minutes. He listened for any sign of movement, but there was nothing, only silence. The room felt empty. Yet there were eyes upon him, and the ambience of the room made his skin crawl. An evil lived here, an evil greater than he could ever imagine. But where? And what was he supposed to do if he found it? He considered wandering around the room in search of a doorway when he stopped.

The floor consisted of huge tiles, alternating black and white across the surface. It very much resembled a chessboard. However, it wasn't the stones that surprised him. In the very center of the floor, a large circular stone lay surrounded by the black and white tiles. He had been standing on it but he hadn't noticed. He couldn't make out the details of the stone in the dim light, so he knelt down to get a closer look.

Two figures stood opposing one another. On one side a tall man all in black fought with a sword of midnight. The sword appeared to eat the light and darken everything around it. A boy stood across from the man in black, a sword of fiery blue in his hands. Their blades were locked in front of them in a struggle in which neither refused to budge. Whoever did would lose, and die.

Wait a moment. That boy. Thomas bent even closer, trying to get a better look at the face carved into the stone. It looked remarkably familiar. In fact, it looked more than familiar. It looked like him! But what could it mean? Why would his image be set into this floor? The answer was so obvious he had missed it. Was his grandfather correct? Was he the Defender of the Light? If so, then the man in black carved into the stone must be—

"So, after all these years, my opponent has finally arrived." The soft words, said with undeniable menace, echoed throughout the chamber. A voice in Thomas' head told him to run, to escape, but it was too late. "I've been waiting a long time for you. A very long time."

Thomas rose to his feet and turned around. A man coalesced out of the shadows, his boots thudding softly on the stone floor. It was as if the image in the circular stone had come to life. The man before him wore midnight black with a long cloak flowing behind him. The hood of the cloak hid the man's face, but the eyes were unmistakable. The pinpricks of red blazed in the darkness. A bolt of fear shot through Thomas, and his hand automatically went to the hilt of his sword. The voice inside his head screamed hysterically, ordering him, then begging him, to run, to get away. But his legs refused to move. The Shadow Lord had come for him.

"Don't look so surprised, boy," said the Shadow Lord as he stalked across the room toward his prey, his voice echoing throughout the chamber. "You should have known it was simply a matter of time; that you were destined to stand across from me one day." The Shadow Lord's words crackled with anticipation, with hunger. Thomas shivered with fear. His greatest nightmare had come to life and now was no more than twenty feet away and fast approaching.

Thomas pulled his sword from its sheath. The few rays of light danced off the blade and burned a path through the shadows that misted and curled about the room. The light disappeared quickly, crushed by the darkness.

The Shadow Lord laughed softly as he continued toward Thomas. "I had hoped that this would be easy, that you would recognize the futility of your efforts." His words sounded like the dry scraping of a snake as it slithered across a jagged, rocky surface. "But we all must live with disappointment."

Thomas breathed deeply, trying to calm himself. Though his fear remained, he had locked it away into a small part of his mind. All of his weapons trainers had told him much the same thing: Fear was common on the field of battle. There was little difference between a great warrior and a competent soldier, except the great warrior recognized his fear and used it to his advantage. The soldier only knew that he was afraid.

If he wanted to survive, he needed to think clearly and move quickly. If his fear got the better of him, he would die. In one fluid movement, the Shadow Lord pulled his sword from beneath his cloak, the steel blacker than the night. The already dim chamber grew darker as the steel absorbed the last few bits of light.

"I hope you've enjoyed your life, Thomas Keldragan Kestrel," said the Shadow Lord. "It's about to end."

The Shadow Lord lunged forward, his blade aimed at Thomas' chest. But Thomas expected the attack and easily sidestepped it.

"So, you won't be easy meat for me today," said the Shadow Lord as he circled back around Thomas. Thomas danced a few feet away, his sword held at the ready. The Shadow Lord's laugh echoed throughout the chamber. "Good. That is very good, Thomas. I could use a little fun today."

The Shadow Lord lunged forward again, arm outstretched, the black blade quivering in anticipation, searching for blood. Thomas avoided the blade and again put a few feet between himself and the Shadow Lord.

"A game of cat and mouse," said the Shadow Lord, watching as Thomas warily stepped around him and moved closer to the stone disk set in the floor. What little light there was in the room illuminated only the center of the chamber, and then only dimly. Even with Thomas' eyesight, he couldn't penetrate the outlying ring of darkness.

Fighting the Shadow Lord was certainly not something Thomas relished, but every one of his instructors had lectured about the need for information. Winning on the battlefield usually did not involve strength or courage or desire, though those factors certainly played a large part in tipping the scales in your favor. No, the key to victory was knowledge.

The same concept applied to single combat, and each of his instructors had counseled that Thomas first learn his opponent's style before committing himself to a course of action. "It would be unfortunate, would it not," Antonin, First Spear of the Carthanians, liked to say, "If you learned your opponent's greatest weakness just as his sword entered your gut."

So Thomas employed the strategy suggested by his many tutors. Wait and watch. See what your opponent will do. If you have the time, why not use it? Then, when you've found your opponent's weaknesses, attack. And then attack again. Keep attacking until you've exploited that weakness, then move on to the next one. And the next, and the next, until you've won.

Thomas leaped to the side, barely avoiding another thrust of the black sword.

"So I must earn my victory today," said the Shadow Lord as he circled Thomas. Thomas moved with him, blade ready in front of him, eyes locked on the red pinpricks glowing within the Shadow Lord's hood. "I never thought an undergrown boy could be so much trouble."

The Shadow Lord feinted forward with his blade, and then pulled back, judging Thomas' reaction. Thomas remained where he was, though his blade shifted reflexively to protect his exposed side. The Shadow Lord now played Thomas' game. Thomas had found what he was looking for. It was time to attack.

Rather than lunging forward, Thomas swung his blade down in an arc, catching the Shadow Lord by surprise. Fiery sparks flew into the air as Thomas' sword crashed heavily upon the black steel. The Shadow Lord tried to disengage, but Thomas wouldn't allow it, pushing the Shadow Lord back as he continued his attack, swinging his blade low, then high, in an effort to keep his opponent off balance.

Each time the two swords met, sparks danced through the air. No matter how aggressively Thomas attacked, the Shadow Lord defended himself. Thomas finally backed away, knowing that it was time to change his tactics.

"A boy with fire," said the Shadow Lord, breathing heavily. Perhaps Thomas had found one of the weaknesses he sought. Remarkably, his fear had left him. In the beginning, it had almost paralyzed him, but now he knew that he could hold his own against the Shadow Lord. "And full of surprises. Well, now it's my turn for a surprise."

The hair along the back of Thomas' neck prickled just before he was knocked through the air and into the far wall of the chamber, landing heavily on the stone floor. Dark Magic! Thomas had focused so much on his swordplay, he had forgotten about the true source of the Shadow Lord's power. As Thomas rose to his feet, another block of air knocked the air from his lungs and slammed him against the wall a second time. Gasping for breath, Thomas seized control of the Talent. He did so just in time, fending off a third blow from the Shadow Lord.

"The cub wants to lead the pack." The Shadow Lord laughed softly. "Let's see if he can." A ball of fire leapt from the Shadow Lord's hand. Using the Talent, Thomas formed a shield of air, deflecting the fireball against the far wall. Another ball of fire flew toward him, and another, and another. Each time Thomas' shield held.

Though Thomas had successfully defended himself thus far, the Shadow Lord's skill and experience with Dark Magic far surpassed his own with the Talent. If he gave the Shadow Lord the opportunity, eventually he would find a weapon that Thomas did not know how to protect against. Not wanting to give the Shadow Lord the chance to continue with his fun, a bolt of white light shot from Thomas' hand.

Surprised by the attack, the Shadow Lord dove out of the

way just in time. Thomas ran forward, aiming his sword at the Shadow Lord's neck. It was extremely difficult to fight with the Talent and a sword at the same time, as both disciplines required absolute concentration. Thomas hoped the same applied to the Shadow Lord, otherwise he stood virtually no chance of making it out of the chamber alive.

Thomas would not make the same mistake again and allow the Shadow Lord to attack. That would only lead to his death. Though Thomas was strong in the Talent, and could use it quite effectively, he was no match in a drawn-out struggle against the Shadow Lord's Dark Magic. Given time, the Shadow Lord's thousands of years of experience would win out.

Thomas attacked relentlessly, his blade almost moving on its own in search of the Shadow Lord's blood. Yet with each stroke of his sword, the Shadow Lord's black blade moved to defend. Several times the Shadow Lord tried to launch another attack with his Dark Magic, but Thomas prevented it by pressing him even harder. The dance around the chamber continued at a furious pace, the two blades crashing against one another in a shower of white sparks.

As time passed, the Shadow Lord's movements became more lethargic, as did Thomas'. The struggle was taking its toll on both of them. Thomas' sword felt heavy in his hands and his knees began to shake. He would not be able to continue his attack for much longer. However, if he stopped, the Shadow Lord would be free to use his Dark Magic. Thomas knew what the inevitable result of that scenario would be. He could use the Talent against the Shadow Lord's attacks, but each time he did so he would become weaker and weaker, until finally he was just a little too slow and the Shadow Lord broke through his defenses. Time was quickly slipping away.

Energized by his need, Thomas redoubled his efforts. Ignoring the strain in his shoulders and arms, his sword was a blur. The Shadow Lord could only deflect the blows, unable to counterattack. Thomas pressed even harder. The Shadow Lord was weakening. Thomas' sword came closer and closer to its intended target.

Seeing his opportunity, Thomas swung his sword in a downward arc with all his strength. The Shadow Lord got his blade up just in time, preventing Thomas' steel from digging into his flesh. This time, though, rather than letting his sword glance off of the Shadow Lord's black steel, he kept the full force of his blow on the upraised steel, inevitably pushing the dark blade downward until it crashed into the floor. The jolt from the blow weakened the Shadow Lord's grip, and with a quick sweep of his blade, Thomas knocked it from the Shadow Lord's hand. Thomas stood before the Shadow Lord, his sword point pressed against the Shadow Lord's chest.

"A good fight," said the Shadow Lord with some difficulty as he struggled for breath, seemingly unaware of the cold death poised just inches from his heart. "For that I will give you a choice." The Shadow Lord's voice remained a soft, cold whisper. The menace within it was clear, though now Thomas sensed something else. Could it be fear?

"I could have snuffed out your life anytime I wanted to," said the Shadow Lord. "Your Talent is no match for my Dark Magic. Even now, I can take your life anytime I want to. But I will give you a choice nonetheless because you are a worthy opponent."

Perhaps that was so. Perhaps the Shadow Lord could have killed him anytime he wanted to. It didn't sound right, though. If he was truly the Defender of Light, the Shadow Lord had waited thousands of years for this moment, waiting thousands of years to kill him, thereby removing the final obstacle to his plans. All he had to do was eliminate Thomas and the King-doms would be his. Nothing else stood in his way.

But instead the Shadow Lord had dueled with him. Just for the fun of it? It was wrong. All wrong. Then again, who could guess how the Shadow Lord's mind worked? Thomas knew the

Shadow Lord could kill him in an instant with his Dark Magic. Of course, in an instant, he could embed his sword in the Shadow Lord's chest. Shadow Lord or no, three inches of steel in his heart would certainly kill him.

"Remove your sword, and you will live," said the Shadow Lord. "Remove your sword, and you will be free of everything. Even from the prophecy. I will not pursue you, and you can live your life as you choose. If you do not, you will die."

Thomas stood there caught by his own indecision. Free from the prophecy? Free from all the burdens of his life? Free to make his own choices rather than having them made for him?

The pinpricks of red that served as the Shadow Lord's eyes burned brightly. Thomas could choose freedom and do what he wanted with his life, but then the Shadow Lord would also be free to do as he wanted as well. Though it appeared to be a simple choice — life or death — it was anything but. The muscles in his shoulders bunched up, preparing to strike. Thomas chose death.

The blinding white light caught Thomas by surprise. When he opened his eyes he was back on the Stone. The Sylvan Warriors still stood in front of the enormous columns. Their expressions remained serious, but their eyes seemed more hopeful to Thomas. For a moment, he thought his battle with the Shadow Lord had been real, and that he had died. Thankfully, it was only one of the dreams. He wondered, though, if there was some truth in each of the dreams he had just navigated. Would he one day have to fight the Shadow Lord? Hold on. The challenges! Was that the final challenge?

"The Sylvana are a people of courage," said Tiro in a voice that rang of victory. "You have chosen correctly."

Thomas grinned at the pronouncement. Rynlin and Rya had both lectured about the importance of remaining silent during the testing. The candidate was not allowed to speak while on the Stone. When Thomas had asked why they had simply said tradition. Nevertheless, Thomas' smile spoke volumes. Tiro's next few words wiped it from his face.

"Each challenge teaches a lesson, and I bid you heed the lesson learned. Remember these three things, and you will join us if you are judged worthy."

Judged worthy? Didn't he just prove he was worthy by overcoming the challenges? From now on he'd demand full explanations from Rynlin and Rya. Their habit of holding something back, usually the most important bit of information, was becoming remarkably irritating.

"First, you must have the inner strength to do what is necessary, even at great personal risk. We protect nature. That responsibility comes before our own lives.

"Second, you must recognize that the choice between right and wrong is never easy, and that doing the right thing can often be more painful than doing the wrong.

"Third, no matter what choice you make there is always a cost."

Thomas listened carefully to Tiro's words. Each dream had taught him one of those lessons, and he knew that he would never forget them. Tiro sounded very much like Rynlin in the way he presented things in that he enjoyed the sound of his own voice. Why should he be surprised? Tiro and Rynlin were probably good friends. Thomas was quickly brought back from his wandering thoughts by Tiro's final pronouncement.

"It is time for the judgment."

12

———

THE JUDGMENT

"You have proven you are a man of action, a man of honor and a man of courage," began Tiro, his wispy hair a victim of the light breeze. "That, however, is not enough to become a Sylvan Warrior. A man or woman cannot make the final judgment. Nature itself must make the judgment. You have heard of the Valley of the Unicorns?"

Thomas nodded. All the time he had spent listening to Rynlin and Rya had finally paid off. The Valley of the Unicorns was for most people a place of fantasy, a legend thousands of years old. The ancient stories named it the home of the unicorns. Supposedly these mythical beasts were actual manifestations of nature — the natural energy given physical form. Other tales, even older than those myths, said unicorns were horses that had come to nature's aid when nature itself was threatened by some long forgotten evil. To thank the horses for their assistance, nature bestowed their horns upon them, which held within them the power of nature.

No one could recall the veracity of these legends, but neither would anyone deny the unicorn's unique closeness to nature. Located just below the Circle, the Valley overlooked the

Breaker. Many adventurers had gone off in search of the Valley of the Unicorns, only to wander around aimlessly in the Highlands. It was said that only a Sylvan Warrior could find the Valley. All others were turned away by the magic of the unicorns. It guaranteed that only those who were supposed to find the valley did so.

The unicorns had a unique relationship with the Sylvana, serving as their steeds in battle. Not every Sylvan Warrior had the skill to master the Talent, and therefore was vulnerable to the Dark Magic of the Shadow Lord. The natural magic of the unicorn protected the Warrior in battle, and for those who could use the Talent, the magic of the unicorn augmented their strength.

It helped to explain why the Sylvan Warriors were such formidable opponents, despite their relatively few numbers. Of course, just like the Sylvan Warriors, unicorns were not immortal. A unicorn died if its horn was removed. And just as the number of Sylvan Warriors had diminished over time because of their fight with the Shadow Lord, so too had the number of unicorns.

Of course, Tiro didn't assume Thomas knew more than just the name. "The Valley of the Unicorns is home to the war horses of the Sylvana. Every animal is a part of nature, but the natural magic flows within these creatures. They are stronger and faster than other horses and can gallop for days without tiring. It is they who will judge you worthy of joining the Sylvana."

Thomas nodded his understanding.

"But be forewarned," continued the portly officiant. "If you are not judged worthy, you will die. You have passed the tests, and once begun they must be completed. Now you have a choice, however. You do not have to enter the Valley. Though you can never become a Sylvan Warrior if you do not, you will leave here alive. Will you risk death to join us? Will you be judged?"

For Thomas little thought was required for his answer. He had come too far to turn back now. He nodded again.

"So be it," intoned Tiro.

With the sweep of an arm, he directed Thomas' gaze to a point just outside the Circle, on the side opposite the forest that had served as part of his first test. When he had arrived, that section of the plain looked just as desolate and uninviting as the rest, trailing off to a steep drop. Now, he saw a steep path leading down to a huge crater with an edge that stretched for leagues around.

Thomas tried to hide his surprise, though he likely did a poor job of it. The Talent could not have hidden the path from him. The strength needed to do that would be enormous, and with Thomas' ability in the Talent, being so close to it would have alerted him. No, it had to be the natural magic of the unicorns. Truly amazing!

"The path will lead you to the Valley. Once there, walk to its very center. Then wait. There you will be judged. This time the choice will be made for you."

Thomas studied the crater a final time before walking slowly down the steps of the Stone, then out of the Circle. Once past the stone columns, he made his way to the path leading down to the crater. Thomas took his time because of the trail's steep slope. After everything he'd been through so far, tripping on the loose rocks and falling to his death was something he wanted to avoid. Gazing back up the slope, the stone columns of the Circle were now just tiny specks poking up above the edge of the plain. He hadn't noticed just how far he had traveled. Finally reaching the lip of the crater, he rested his hands on the large rocks that formed the rim. To his left, the path continued on into the Valley.

It truly was a remarkable sight, one that Thomas had never

expected for a place as forbidding as the Highlands. Snuggled in the very middle of the highest peak in the Highlands sat a valley of lush green grass that appeared to stretch on forever. The grass resembled the waves of the ocean as it followed the commands of the wind. The only break in the green landscape was a sparkling river that ran along one side of the valley. A strong gust of cold wind sent shivers through Thomas' body. Taking it as a sign that he should get moving, he ventured down into the Valley of the Unicorns.

That was odd. As he stepped between the rocks and down into the crater, he discovered that there were no trees. And where were the unicorns? All he could see, all the way to the other edge of the crater, was the tall, green grass flowing in the wind. What he found even stranger was the temperature. With each step, the air felt warmer. A gentle breeze wafted across the valley floor and sucked the cold from him. When he set foot on the floor of the crater, he thought he had walked into an early spring, a far cry from the chilly autumn that waited for him at the crater's rim.

Breathing deeply of the spring-scented air, Thomas started his journey to the center of the valley. The warm weather brightened his spirits and reinvigorated him. The exhaustion that had crept into his body because of the tests slowly dissipated, replaced by a renewed energy. As he walked slowly through the tall grass, the age of the valley enveloped him. A wisdom lived here, a knowledge, thousands of years old. From that knowledge came a serenity that filled Thomas with a sense of peace and tranquility. Yet, instead of feeling old, there was a vibrancy to the valley. Life undulated all around him, though he could see nothing of it.

The contradictions teased at Thomas' awareness. Then he had it. Nature, or rather its contradictions. At one moment old, at another young. At one moment reserved, at another wild. It was all part of the cycle of death and regeneration. Thomas sensed that the Valley of the Unicorns was the center of all nature. He had virtually no evidence to support his theory, but every fiber of his being knew it was true.

The excitement he had felt upon first entering the Valley gave way to a calm he had never experienced before. He was at peace with himself for the first time in his short life. All his burdens melted away, replaced by a freedom that promised happiness and fulfillment. Even the stinging sensation from his scraped palms and aching muscles disappeared. Looking down at his hands, the scratches and cuts had healed.

After walking for more than an hour through the tall grass, Thomas judged that he had reached the center of the valley. Coming to a stop, he spun around slowly, looking for any type of movement. As before, only the tall grass responding to the whims of the wind was visible. Still, he felt strange eyes on him. Sensing no danger, however, Thomas let the feeling of life wash over him, enjoying the calm. Several times he glanced around, feeling more and more eyes watching him. Yet each time he saw nothing and shrugged it off.

Closing his eyes, Thomas breathed in deeply. The Valley nearly overwhelmed him with its serenity. When he opened his eyes a few minutes later, he almost fell to the ground in shock. Dozens of unicorns surrounded him. Black, white, roan, even a few with spotted brown and white coats, stared at him with ancient eyes. The eyes he had felt were real.

The unicorns had arrayed themselves around him in a loose circle, studying him closely. Thomas took a moment to examine these beautiful creatures as well, which until that very moment had been nothing more than stories to him. The pictures he had seen in history books were wrong. They showed animals no bigger than goats, with one small horn rising from their foreheads. These unicorns dwarfed the draft horses used by traders and merchants. The shoulder of the smallest unicorn easily surpassed Thomas' height, and the horns rose seven to eight feet into the air. The biggest unicorn, one whose height at the shoulder probably matched that of Catal Huyuk, had a horn that looked to be at least nine feet long.

From the majesty of their appearance, Thomas understood why they were considered the lords of the wild. Their strength and power were apparent in their forms. Several times Thomas had to remind himself to breathe. The unicorns were the most beautiful animals he had ever seen. The life, the passion, the power of nature appeared clearly within them. Protecting that goodness from evil, and preserving it for the future, was the worthiest cause he could imagine.

Tiro had said that the unicorns would judge him, but how that would occur he didn't know. Rynlin explained to him once that each member of the Sylvana was paired with a unicorn. Once selected, that steed served as that Sylvan Warrior's warhorse until either one died. How that related to the judgment he wasn't sure.

Unicorns had a natural ability to look into the heart of a person or animal. That was another reason they were so effective in the battle against the Shadow Lord, who had tried to deceive the Sylvana many times in the past, but to no avail. Though these deceptions sometimes worked on Sylvan Warriors since they were, after all, human and vulnerable to man's normal frailties, the unicorn did not have such a weakness.

Rynlin once told him the story of one of the first Sylvan Warriors, a young woman named Aine. She was given the task of guarding a small pass that led through the Charnel Mountains and out onto the Northern Steppes. The Dark Horde had risen once again and was moving toward the south. The bulk of that hideous army was expected to move through the larger passes. However, the Shadow Lord knew the Sylvana would be prepared for such an advance, so he sent several hundred

Ogren and Shades through the tiny pass, which was known as Dagger's Gap. While the Sylvana were occupied with his main army, this group would attack from behind, allowing the main force to break into the southlands.

Dagger's Gap was so called for the most obvious of reasons; it resembled a dagger, with a large opening at one end that narrowed down to a point. Aine made her stand at the tip of the blade. Because of the size of the Gap there, a single warrior could hold at bay a much larger enemy force for quite a long time. In an attempt to get past the lone Sylvan Warrior, the Shadow Lord used his Dark Magic to give the Shades and Ogren that approached Aine the appearance of Sylvan Warriors.

Though Aine did not see through the deception, the unicorn that served as her mount, a golden white female named Veritas, which in the old tongue translated to "Truth," charged the first Ogren to walk through Dagger's Gap. Aine tried desperately to stop Veritas, but was too slow, and she watched in horror as the unicorn lowered its head and aimed its horn at the image of one of her friends. As the unicorn's magical horn pierced the Ogren's chest, it destroyed the Shadow Lord's spell, and Aine saw the true enemy before her. With the help of Veritas, she held Dagger's Gap until a contingent of Sylvan Warriors came to her aid.

Thomas gave a start as a fleeting tendril of consciousness touched his mind. It felt very much like when he spoke with Beluil or another animal of the forest. Yet, the unicorns had initiated it. Thinking that the judgment had begun, Thomas opened his mind to the contact. Immediately the thoughts and feelings of the dozens of unicorns standing around him bombarded his mind.

The tremendous age and wisdom of each animal drifted into his consciousness, searching his heart for weakness. After recovering from the initial flood of disparate emotions and personalities, unable to resist the temptation, Thomas pushed out his own mind, strengthening his connection to the unicorns. By doing so, he could see the natural magic flowing all around him, though he could not distinguish its primary source — nature itself or the unicorns.

Dazzled by it all, Thomas extended his senses even more, trying to link more closely with the magic that waxed and waned around him. As he did so, he felt a tie begin to form between him and the unicorns, a bond stronger than any he could imagine, one that went to the very depths of his soul. His necklace grew warmer against his skin as the bond grew stronger, solidifying and becoming something tangible. Ever so slowly the unicorns tied themselves to him. As a result, Thomas was bound to nature itself more deeply than he had ever thought possible. Remarkably, the bond did not weigh him down as some of his other burdens did. Instead, he saw the bond for what it really was — a gift.

Just as quickly as the bond formed, it disappeared, as did his contact with the unicorns. An overwhelming sense of loss filled Thomas at the abrupt break. He had never known such comfort and security before, and he longed for it to continue. Despite the break, the unicorns remained around him, watching closely with their large eyes, once wary, now friendly and open. Thomas waited with bated breath for several seconds to see what would happen next. Much to his surprise, a single unicorn stepped forward and walked toward him at a stately pace.

13

DARKBANE

The tall, black unicorn stood before him, holding itself with a dignity rarely seen in any other creature. The unicorn examined Thomas, weighing him with its eyes. Thomas stared back, amazed by the wisdom of the ages held there. The unicorn nodded quickly, the strong muscles rippling in its neck. The movement resembled one of Rynlin's nods of approval. Ever so slowly the unicorn bent its head until its jet-black horn stopped only inches from Thomas' chest.

Thomas marveled at the design of the creature's horn, fascinated by the spiral that began at the base where it sat atop the unicorn's head to where it ended as a sharp point. A jolt of recognition shot through him. The carving on the necklace he wore, the one his grandfather gave him during his escape from the Crag. He had forgotten about it, but now it all came flooding back to him. As the unicorn's horn edged closer, the necklace changed from warm to hot, as the carving it held responded to the proximity of the natural magic within the black stallion's horn.

Cautiously, Thomas extended his fingers toward the ebony horn. When he was just about to touch it, he drew his fingers back, still unsure of what would happen next. Had he passed the judgment, or was this simply the final step for failing? Thomas banished the thought from his mind. The unicorn recognized his hesitation and whinnied softly. Taking it as encouragement to continue, Thomas slowly stretched out his fingers until they lightly touched the tip of the unicorn's horn. With that one touch the flurry of emotions, images and thoughts that surged through the contact almost consumed him. The inside of his skull felt like it was going to explode, but thankfully the stream of consciousness became more manageable. All of Thomas' memories, all of his thoughts and beliefs, even all of his secrets and fears, mixed with those of the unicorn.

Thomas felt the bond taking shape. He imagined it to be a thin cord of steel slowly tying itself around himself and the black unicorn standing before him. The coil of steel had a life of its own, twisting and turning according to the instructions of a voice that only it could hear in such a way that the knot could never become unraveled. As the minutes slowly passed the cord of steel increased in size. It began with the thickness of a piece of hair, until it was almost as thick as his wrist.

Pictures flew through Thomas' mind at a dizzying pace. He quickly realized that this magnificent creature was actually several hundred years old. In the next memory he was able to decipher, the unicorn galloped toward a small group of Ogren and Shades, its head lowered and its horn sticking out like a lance, with the Breaker in the background. Thomas felt the steed's pleasure in its charge, and the rush of adrenaline as it crashed into the dark creatures, its rider laying about with a huge two-handed sword. The images continued to flash through his mind, many so fast that Thomas could not figure them out, yet they remained within him nonetheless, becoming a part of his own consciousness.

Thomas saw the unicorn's naming as it came of age —

Acero, meaning strength or steel in the Old Tongue. It was a good name, Thomas thought, and matched the unicorn well. The scenes continued to flash through his mind until finally there were no more to view. The unicorn's entire life had passed before Thomas' eyes. He was awed by it all and honored for the privilege.

Then the process reversed itself. Acero began to unravel Thomas' memories, and the images of his life, many locked away even from himself, burst forth. The fight in the Burren played out once again. Thomas' sword sweeping off the head of the second Ogren filled the unicorn with pride. Many of the images passed by in a blur, from Thomas' training sessions with both weapons and the Talent to taking the Sword of the Highlands in his small hands for the first time before making his way through the secret tunnel beneath the Crag to safety, Acero absorbing it all. A lump formed in Thomas' throat as the last image appeared. Thomas saw himself looking into the flashing green eyes of a beautiful woman, her chestnut hair matted to her face by perspiration. He guessed that it was his mother, and it brought an ache of grief to his heart.

Then, as quickly as it began, the sharing ended. Rubbing his head slightly, Thomas was shocked that he could take in so much so fast. He knew everything there was to know about Acero, and the unicorn knew the same about him. As he looked into the eyes of the magnificent beast, they held a smile of friendship. Thomas stepped toward Acero and almost fell, surprised to find that his legs were weak from what had just happened.

Acero instead moved toward him and motioned with his head.

"Thank you, my friend. I would be honored." Taking hold of the Acero's muscular neck, Thomas pulled himself up onto his broad back.

The unicorn then turned and began walking across the

Valley toward the steep path leading back up to the Circle. The other unicorns gracefully stepped aside, allowing the two to pass. As they did so, each unicorn bowed its head. It reminded Thomas of what a knight would do in ancient times if the lord or king passed. He couldn't understand why these ancient, powerful beasts would do the same for him. He didn't think he had yet earned such respect, or ever could.

As he passed through the herd, images drifted through his mind, resulting from the tentative touches of the other unicorns. They had seen something within him during the judgment, something that Thomas had not yet seen himself. It only confirmed his worst fears.

Darkbane. Darkbane. The word slipped through Thomas' mind as he passed by one unicorn, only to return as he neared another. *Darkbane. Darkbane. Darkbane.* When Acero finally reached the path leading out of the valley, the thoughts of the unicorns receded, giving Thomas a much-needed respite. Yet, no matter how hard he tried, one remained. *Darkbane.*

14

FOUND WORTHY

Acero, with Thomas on his back, pranced into the Circle, kicking his legs up high and holding his head back in pride. He had found a new rider after decades of waiting, and one worthy of his abilities. As Acero neared the Stone he slowed his pace. The unicorn walked slowly around it, allowing each Sylvan Warrior to view Thomas. Smiles and grins replaced their stony expressions. Rya even had a tear in her eye.

After circling the Stone, Thomas jumped off of Acero's back and gave him a thankful pat on the neck before walking up the worn steps. Tiro waited there for him. Even he had a smile on his face.

"Please kneel." Thomas settled onto one knee. "You have been found worthy to join us, Thomas Keldragan Kestrel," declared Tiro, the pomposity that had echoed across the plain replaced with pride, as if he had had something to do with Thomas' success.

Reaching into one of the many pockets of his voluminous brown robes, the portly sorcerer pulled out a length of silver that shined brightly in the sunlight. He then placed the silver necklace carefully over Thomas' head. Thomas did not have to look at it to know what it was. The necklace matched the one he already wore, with the long silver chain supporting the medallion upon which an intricately carved unicorn's horn gleamed brightly. A feeling of warmth spread through him as the metal touched his skin. This was his own necklace, one that he had earned himself.

"We are fewer in number than in years past, but our responsibilities have not diminished," said Tiro, his didactic voice carrying to the far reaches of the mountaintop. The Sylvan Warrior loved to hear himself talk and was enjoying himself immensely at the moment. "The battle between good and evil continues, and we must stand ready, for we are the only ones who can keep the darkness from covering the Kingdoms. We must stand ready to defend against the Shadow Lord and his servants."

Thomas remained kneeling as Tiro spoke. He felt at peace with himself. He had wanted to join the Sylvana ever since Rynlin's first lesson about them. And he had succeeded. He was a Sylvan Warrior.

Thomas swept his gaze over the other Sylvan Warriors, memorizing their faces. He was one of them now and had accepted the responsibilities that Tiro now spoke of as his own. When Tiro mentioned the Shadow Lord, the smiles disappeared from the faces of the Sylvana. Some of their expressions became more determined, some angry. A few even looked hungry, as if they would welcome such a clash. He could understand why. It would give them the opportunity to do what they were born to do, what he was born to do as well. He knew that now. He had finally found where he belonged.

As Thomas studied his new companions, he saw something else as well. Something he had missed during his earlier examination. For thousands of years the Sylvana had fought the Shadow Lord, yet during that time they had never defeated him. Well, that wasn't exactly true. They had defeated him, but they had never destroyed him. They had prevented him from sweeping down to the south from his bastion in the Charnel Mountains innumerable times, but they had played the game over and over and had never before had the ability to do more than defend. They had repeatedly defeated his forces and removed him as a threat to the Kingdoms, for a time.

The reason why they had never done more was quite simple. They had never before had a weapon they could use to defeat the Shadow Lord once and for all. Until now. He saw it in their eyes. A sudden knowledge took root in his mind, and it terrified him. It filled him with a sense of dread that buried itself deep within his heart. They saw *him* as that weapon. They saw *him* as their means to victory. Duty and responsibility weighed him down as never before.

Thomas beat back the growing panic within him. He could be wrong. Maybe he was simply misreading the situation. *Darkbane. Darkbane.* The words passed through his mind. The unicorns had read his heart, his very soul. They had judged him worthy to join the Sylvana, but had they judged him worthy of something else as well? They had called him Darkbane. The term left little to the imagination.

When Tiro had placed the medallion around his neck just minutes before, Thomas had felt for the first time in his life that he was in control, that he could make decisions without having to worry all the time about what he was supposed to do. That precious control had just been ripped painfully from his hands, and he felt as if he were hurtling along a steep and sliding trail blindfolded. Where he would end up he didn't know, and that only increased his fear. The reality of his situation became crystal clear.

Joining the Sylvana had never really been a true choice, it had simply been just one more thing he was supposed to do. *You must do what you must do.* Rya's words of wisdom now sounded more and more like a curse. Thomas promised himself that one of these days he would have a choice, one that he could actually make, rather than being pushed and pulled in various directions by the prophecies or some greater force. One day he would choose how to live his life, regardless of the consequences.

"Acero has judged you worthy," continued Tiro. The unicorn rose on his hind legs and neighed shrilly at the mention of his name, proud to be in the Circle once more. Acero could sense that Thomas was special, even if the boy did not yet know it. That filled him with a pride and sense of purpose he had not known for more than two hundred years. "When the time comes for us to fight, he will be your steed."

Tiro again pulled something from his robes, but held it behind his back. "The necklace you have just received ties you to us. It can never be removed from your neck while you live. If there is ever a time you are in need, we will know, and we will come." That explained a great deal for Thomas. Now he knew why he could take the necklace given to him by his grandfather on and off his neck at will. It had been a gift and was not truly his.

Tiro then handed him a golden horn curled once around in a circle. It was a very simple design with little ornamentation. The only way to identify it from any other horn was the mark running along the metal near the mouthpiece. The unicorn's lance, just as it was carved into his amulet.

"This is one of the Horns of the Sylvana. Once, all the rulers of the Kingdoms used them to summon us during a time of great need. Those days are over, and the Horns have been taken from those who care more for wealth and power than for the welfare of those they are duty-bound to protect. Use it wisely. This functions much like the necklace. Blow on it three times. We will hear. We will come. We will conquer. Woe to any who stand before us." The bitterness at the failures of the Kingdoms remained for Tiro. Thomas didn't doubt that many other Sylvan Warriors felt the same way.

In Thomas' opinion their feelings were justified. Based on everything he had learned of the Sylvana from Rynlin and Rya, as well as a few more objective resources, the Sylvan Warriors had once been a great ally to the Kingdoms. That had changed with the Great War when the political squabbles of the different Kingdoms almost led to their own downfall and the needless deaths of many Sylvan Warriors. The Sylvana withdrew from the affairs of man because of it.

The power of the Sylvan Horns was legendary. Thomas even remembered a story that involved one of his relatives, the Highland Lord a few generations before his grandfather. Though the Sylvana had taken most of the Horns from the Kingdoms, at the time a few had remained with those rulers not blinded by personal ambition and greed. The Highland Lord had traveled through the Highlands and out onto the Northern Steppes to confirm reports of forays by the creatures of the Shadow Lord into his kingdom. After he and his men had marched a few leagues beyond the safety of the Highlands, several thousand Ogren and Shades making their way south ambushed them. The Highland Lord did his best to hold them off, but his hundred or so men could only do so much against a force several thousand strong. In desperation, he blew three times on the Horn of the Sylvana. The three strong notes echoed across the Northern Steppes and the Highlands, and beyond, but he had already lost half of his men and held little hope for survival.

Those soldiers still able to resist the onslaught had formed a tight circle around his banner, fighting ferociously against the Ogren and Shades, but they knew it was only a matter of time. Much to the Highland Lord's surprise, only a few seconds after he had pressed his lips to the Horn, far off in the distance he heard an answering cry. A second note then came from the west, clearer and stronger than the first. The Highland Lord tried to rally his men and give them hope of rescue, but the overwhelming number of Ogren and Shades pressed in on all sides.

Then a third note sounded, even stronger and clearer than the previous two. The sound caused the earth to shake and the wind to howl, and as it lingered in the air, the rumble of hooves echoed across the Northern Steppes. A misty cloud suddenly formed around the battlefield and from its midst charged the Sylvana, bolts of fire and lightning shooting out from the sorcerers among them, blasting into the Ogren and Shades that dared to venture from the Charnel Mountains. It must have been a magnificent sight, Thomas thought. Tiro's voice broke through his daydreaming.

"As you know, each Sylvan Warrior is given charge of a particular land, and we now give you one that has lacked our assistance for almost a century. Rise, Thomas Keldragan Kestrel, and take your place among us as a Sylvan Warrior. The safety and freedom of the Highlands falls to you."

Cheers rang out from the Sylvan Warriors arrayed below him as Thomas rose to his feet. He felt the warmth of his new necklace brush against his chest. In a way, it felt like a new chain of added responsibility choking off his freedom, yet strangely he also experienced a new sense of purpose. Maybe he could do more with his life rather than focusing strictly on revenge and winning back something that he still didn't know if he wanted.

Darkbane. Darkbane. Unbidden, the name ran through his mind. *Darkbane. Darkbane. Darkbane stands on high. Darkbane. Darkbane stands on high.* Thomas turned to the north, unable to resist the urge to do so. From his vantage point, he could just make out the tips of the Charnel Mountains peeking over the horizon. Though a small part of his mind screamed in denial, refusing to accept it, Thomas knew the truth deep within his heart. It was as if a part of his mind, which had remained closed to him up until now, had suddenly sprung open. With it came a frightening recognition and a new knowledge.

Rynlin had been right. The words of the prophecy streaked through his consciousness, mixing with his one overwhelming thought: *When a child of life and death, stands on high, drawn by faith, he shall hold the key to victory in his hand. Darkbane. Swords of fire echo in the burned rock, balancing the future on their blades. Darkbane. Darkbane. Light dances with dark, green fire burns in the night, hopes and dreams follow the wind, to fall in black or white. Darkbane. Darkbane. Darkbane.*

He was Darkbane. He knew it in the very core of his being, and there wasn't anything he could do about it. The course of his life had already been decided, and no matter how he tried to change it, the way his life would end had already been determined. He was the Defender of the Light. A whisper tickled his ear, one that he could barely make out, but he knew its source: *The time has come. Let the duel begin.* Thomas focused on the whisper, struggling vainly to hear more, hoping for some clue as to what would happen next. But there was only silence.

Thomas spun around as footsteps pounded up the Stone. Rya arrived first and gave him a hug, tears of joy visible in her eyes. Rynlin then gave him a few claps on the back, his pride obvious in the huge smile he wore. Rynlin was not one for displaying his emotions, except his anger of course, so Thomas appreciated the gesture.

"You never said it would be so difficult," said Thomas.

Rya pulled away from him, wiping her eyes on her sleeve. She hated getting emotional, especially in front of others.

"We thought it would be best if you didn't know," said Rynlin. "The tests require more in the way of reaction than thinking. The less you think, the more you function naturally. To pass the tests you must follow your instincts. If we had warned you beforehand, you might still be thinking about what choice to make." Rynlin smiled wickedly. "We were quite concerned for a time. You seemed quite taken with the girl. Quite taken with her, indeed. What was her name? Kaylie?"

Thomas flushed with embarrassment. So the Sylvana had seen everything. His ears and face turned bright red.

"Don't let your grandfather's teasing get to you," said Rya, giving her husband a sharp elbow to the midsection. Rynlin had expected it, but couldn't avoid it because of the limited space on the Stone. Tiro had walked down as soon as he had declared Thomas a Sylvan Warrior, but even with him gone, it was crowded with Rynlin and Rya up there with him.

"It all comes down to must, doesn't it?" asked Thomas. "It always seems like we have a choice, when much of the time we really don't."

"Yes, it does," replied Rynlin, rubbing his side where Rya's elbow had connected. After hundreds of years of marriage, she knew his weak spots. "Often we don't have a choice. The difference comes, though, in that most people don't have the courage to do what they must. Sylvan Warriors, you, don't have that option. Whether or not you actually have a choice really doesn't matter. The only thing that matters is that you do what you must. You might not like what you have to do, but you will do it nonetheless."

Leave it to Rynlin to work in a lesson when they were supposed to be celebrating. Thomas' mood suddenly darkened. "You know?"

"Yes, we know," said Rynlin, his expression almost sad. "We'll deal with that later. Come." Rynlin guided Thomas toward the steps. "It's time for you to meet the others."

As Rynlin and Rya led him down the steps and into the throng of well wishers waiting for him, Thomas tried to remember all the names, but his heart wasn't in it. His attention was focused on something else: *The time has come. Let the duel begin.*

15

WARMING COLD STONE

A beam of sunlight had again trespassed, making its way past the clouds over Blackstone and shining brightly through the darkened dome of glass situated on top of the largest building in the empty city. This time, though, the ray of light had little trouble fighting its way through the darkness as the shadows drifted back in fear.

The sunlight struck the chamber in its very center, giving life to a large stone disk surrounded by huge tiles of black and white. On the disk, two figures battled — one a boy holding a sword of white, another a man covered in black with a sword darker than the darkest night.

The ray of sunlight settled there, warming the cold stone. As the seconds passed it grew brighter and brighter and stretched out over the floor, pushing its way into the corners of the chamber and driving away the murk. It continued to advance until the blinding light consumed the room.

It was then that the earth began to shake. A soft rumble at first that increased in intensity. The dust that had settled onto the black and white stones danced in the light for the first time in centuries. The soft rumble became a roar as the columns ringing the edge of the room and buttressing the ceiling moved to the rhythm of the earth.

The quaking became more violent, making the hundred-ton columns sway back and forth as if they were no more than stalks of wheat guided by the wind, until it finally moved outward, spreading through the broken city on the darkened cliff face and out into the mountains, and from there across the Northern Steppes and beyond.

Then just as quickly as it had started, it was over. The earth became silent once more, and the bright ray of light returned to its home above the clouds. But the dust remained, swirling around in the darkness that had returned with an energy it had not experienced in centuries.

16

A LEADER MUST EMERGE

The afternoon passed in a blur of faces and conversation for Thomas as he talked with each Sylvan Warrior. Keeping track of all the names was a difficult task, but Rya stayed at his shoulder and helped him along. As the sun began to set, Catal Huyuk and Daran Sharban started a large fire to ward off the chill. Rya stepped forward then with Elisia and Aurelia Valeran and made a delicious stew in the largest pot Thomas had ever seen. Where it had come from he didn't know.

As the smells from the cook pot wafted out over the Circle, the desire for conversation decreased, replaced by hunger. Thomas, for one, was starved, and he was not alone. Finding a place next to Rynlin on one of the logs that some of the Sylvan Warriors had pulled close to the fire, he gratefully accepted a bowl of stew from his grandmother.

"Were the images real?" he asked Rynlin between bites. Vegetable stew. One of his grandmother's specialties.

"Do you ever run out of questions?" Rynlin was also hungry, and therefore irritable. Thomas should have sat on the other side of the fire, but then he would be near Tiro, and he'd have to listen to him ramble on about something of little interest.

"No, not usually." Thomas sensed his grandfather's reluctance to talk, but pressed forward anyway. "Were the images real?"

"You mean the dreams with the choices?"

Thomas nodded. "Yes, were they real?"

"In part," said Rynlin, digging into his bowl for the last few bites of his stew.

"That doesn't really help me very much," said Thomas, slightly annoyed. Sometimes trying to get an answer out of his grandfather was like pulling teeth.

"What I mean is yes and no."

"Rynlin—"

"Patience, Thomas. Let me explain." Rynlin set his empty bowl down next to the log. Now that he had finished his meal, he could move on to his second favorite task -- teaching. "As you've probably guessed, those dreams were created with the Talent, and in part came from within you. In order to ensure that the choices you had to make meant something to you, they had to be formed from what you cared about most."

Thomas nodded his understanding. "Will they ever come true?"

Rynlin shrugged his shoulders. "Maybe. Some of us have had our dreams come true in their entirety, but I don't know how often that happens. Sometimes only parts of the dreams come true. Sometimes none of it." Rynlin grinned wickedly. "Looking for another kiss, are you?"

Rynlin often could be relentless in his teasing, but he was also smart. As soon as the words left his mouth, he glanced around quickly to make sure his wife was still occupied at the fire. One elbow to the ribs earlier in the day had been enough for him.

Thomas blushed slightly. That had not been his main

reason for asking, though it certainly was a pleasant memory. Unfortunately, he had been thinking more about the third dream. The one that knotted his stomach in fear every time he remembered the feel of the Dark Magic erupting within his body, the feel of his life draining away as he pushed his sword through the Shadow Lord's chest, and then discovering to his horror that he had wasted his life because steel couldn't kill the Shadow Lord.

Thomas wanted to talk to Rynlin about that, but didn't get the opportunity. As soon as the meal ended, the discussion began. The Shadow Lord stirred once again, and they all knew the inevitable result of that.

"We know what the future holds," Tiro said. "The Shadow Lord will strike once more. The question is, with our reduced numbers, will we be able to stand against him as we have in the past?"

"Of course we will," replied Loki Jereil, a tall Sylvan Warrior who wore the robes of a sorcerer over his sparse frame. He was relatively young compared to the other Sylvana, having seen only three hundred summers. But he was old enough to remember fighting at the Breaker during the Great War. Thomas had enjoyed speaking with him for a few moments during the afternoon. Though his short beard was flecked with grey, his eyes retained their youth. "We have stood against him before, and we will again."

"I have no doubt of that," said Tiro. "I wonder instead whether we will hold this time. The size of the Dark Horde continues to grow, while our numbers decrease."

"Tiro, we don't need any predictions of doom from you," said a massively muscled Sylvan Warrior whose sun-darkened skin matched the deep brown of his leather armor. Thomas thought his name was Jeran Caffalyn, from somewhere near the western edge of the Grasslands, but he wasn't sure. Even with Rya's assistance, he couldn't remember everyone's name.

"I am simply throwing out the possibility," said Tiro, raising his voice to make his point. "We must be prepared for every eventuality."

Tiro chattered on for several minutes, though Thomas no longer listened. Tiro seemed to be doing most of the talking, yet he clearly wasn't a leader among the Sylvana. In fact, there didn't seem to be a leader at all. Rather, decisions were made based upon the majority. Rynlin didn't even bother to speak up. Thomas could understand why Rynlin often returned from these meetings so frustrated. Rule by committee certainly wasn't the way to get things done during a crisis.

"I think we must focus on what we know," interrupted Maden, bringing the discussion back to the primary topic. He was almost as tall as Rynlin, and he too had a great deal of skill in the Talent. Unlike other sorcerers, though, he chose to wear leggings and a jacket, and a sword hung at his hip, though it now rested against his knee as he sat near the fire. He could have been as intimidating as Catal Huyuk, but his ready smile prevented it. "Daran has reported more activity along the edges of the Charnel Mountains, and Catal Huyuk has spoken of the dark creatures becoming bolder. Even Elisia and Aurelia have dealt with Ogren for the first time in two hundred years in the mountains of Kashel. The time for battle will be upon us soon."

Rynlin murmured his agreement. "Maden is right. The Shadow Lord will strike soon, perhaps sooner than we think." The finality of Rynlin's words filled Thomas with dread. Being named Darkbane was one thing. Actually proving it was quite another. "In the past, we have always succeeded in defeating the Shadow Lord, but I think that term — defeated — is deceptive."

"What do you mean by that?" interrupted Tiro. The portly sorcerer had a hard time remaining silent. In his own mind, he always had something of value to say.

"I mean yes, we defeated the Dark Horde and prevented it from ravaging the Kingdoms. But we have never defeated the

Shadow Lord. We have only delayed him." Many Sylvana nodded their agreement. During the discussions, Thomas quickly discovered that most of the Sylvan Warriors deferred to Maden and Rynlin. They were the closest thing the Sylvana had to leaders. "Yes, we are fewer in number than ever before, but we should not allow that to restrict us when it comes time to act. Perhaps this time events will turn out differently."

Rynlin gave his grandson a meaningful look to punctuate his words, and one that was not lost on the other Sylvan Warriors. Thomas' feeling of dread increased.

"At the moment, there is little we can do but wait," said Maden, shifting slightly on his log. "I propose, though, that we send regular patrols into the Charnel Mountains. That might give us early warning when the Shadow Lord attacks. It could be in the next few months, or the next few years; regardless, I want to be ready."

Many Sylvana shouted their approval for the idea. They were warriors first and foremost. They all knew the advantages of surprise, particularly with an opponent as deadly as the Shadow Lord.

"Will the Kingdoms stand with us?" asked Tiro. "If they don't, can we hold?"

The two simple questions touched off an explosion of argument. Thomas listened to it all, surprised at the vehemence of some of the Warriors. For several minutes the verbal battle raged. Some Sylvan Warriors argued for warning the Kingdoms and enlisting their aid, while others just as strongly voiced their opinions that the Kingdoms would not listen and would not care. What had started out as a calm discussion degenerated into a shouting match. The arguments continued until one of the twins, Aurelia he thought, spoke up.

"I'm sure the Kingdoms would listen if we rode up to the gates of Eamhain Mhacha and blew them apart." Her words were met with chuckles of laughter that helped to tone down the discussion, though the arguments continued.

Thomas was surprised by what was going on. He had always thought that the Sylvana were a dignified people, and above such things as petty disagreements. Rynlin easily interpreted his expression.

"They are Sylvan Warriors," said Rynlin, leaning over to whisper in his ear. "But they are also men and women. Like other men and women, they often fall prey to their own egos, misperceptions and fears."

Thomas continued to listen to the verbal sparring for more than an hour, until it finally petered out with nothing really decided. The Sylvana would watch and wait. When the attack came they would be ready to defend at the Breaker as they had in the past.

For some reason, that strategy bothered him. Maybe it was his youth getting in the way of reason. Yet, waiting for an attack didn't seem like the surest path to victory. After the gathering broke up, the Sylvana made their way back into the forest to their separate camps. Thomas followed along behind Rynlin and Rya, who were deep in discussion. Though their voices were muffled, he picked up a few words.

"A leader must emerge," Rya said to Rynlin, her arms crossed over her chest because of the cold.

"Yes, but it's too soon. That's not something that can be forced. It will have to be worked out in its own time."

Usually, when Rynlin and Rya whispered when he was around, it never led to anything good. This time whatever they were talking about didn't seem to apply to him. At least he hoped it didn't.

17

———————

BRINGING THE CHAINS

Once the foothills were the breadbasket of the Highlands, providing more than enough food for the people who populated the rugged land. Yet, this bountiful region now bore the scars of war. The burned-out husks of farmhouses had replaced once thriving orchards and fields of wheat and barley. Known for its rich bounty only a few years before, it had become the most obvious symbol of the collapse of Highland power. Although the Highlanders were still the most feared warriors in all the Kingdoms, their numbers were dwindling at a rapid rate.

Much of the responsibility for that fact lay at the feet of Lord Johin Killeran. He was, actually, quite proud of it. Normally a practical people, these warriors vainly hoped that the true heir to the throne of the Highlands — the Lost Kestrel — would return. The Highlanders saw this boy — the Lost Whelp, as Killeran liked to call him — as their savior, who could give them back the freedom they had lost when the Crag fell. Killeran had a much keener insight than most into the question of whether the boy lord still lived. He knew the truth of the matter. The Lost Kestrel was only a myth.

Yet, that did not keep the Highlanders from hoping for a miracle. And he did admire their persistence, though it was wasted effort. But enough was enough. It was time for them to admit that they were a conquered people and to begin acting as such. He had enough to do as it was without having to worry about bands of Marchers coming down from the higher passes to harass his men.

As he saw it, he was only doing his duty. If he had a natural prejudice against the Highlanders, well, they had only themselves to blame. If they had done as he had ordered — asked, really — he would not have been forced to take such extreme measures. Didn't these Marchers understand the pressures he faced as the Regent of the Highlands?

Once the Marchers realized that they could not save the Crag from the surprise attack, they had begun a rearguard action to allow as many people as possible to escape into the mountains, where his men dared not follow. After the destruction of the Crag, Killeran had gained marginal control of the lower Highlands. Though lesser in number, the Highlanders still controlled the higher passes.

The Marchers blended into the forest as if they were a part of it, striking swiftly and then disappearing. Their anger at the loss of their Highland Lord, their homes, their families, their freedom, only served to fuel their rage. Fighting a Marcher was deadly enough. Taking on an angry Marcher was suicidal. Then again, Killeran didn't really have to worry about that. He didn't actually have to fight the Marchers himself — one of the prizes of leadership.

In the beginning, the Marchers were no more than minor annoyances, coming down from the mountains to hound his men and hinder his mining operation. He had hoped that they would stay in their villages, satisfied that they still controlled a portion of their beloved Highlands. Killeran wiped his hand underneath his rather large nose, using his shirtsleeve as a handkerchief. He had suffered colds and chills ever since he came to this cursed land. Ah, well. There was no sense in wishing for an impossibility. He could think of no more difficult people than the Highlanders. Stubborn and strong-willed to a fault, they refused to admit defeat.

The High King had named him Regent seven years before, giving him charge of the Highlands to rule as he saw fit until Rodric assumed control as the law allowed. That day was only three years away. The rulers of the other Kingdoms had acquiesced to his selection, as most viewed him as a neutral party. Why would a Dunmoorian lord care about the Highlands? They were always more interested in acquiring lands by the border with Armagh.

That misguided perspective, and the fact that virtually none of the other rulers demonstrated much concern about the fate of Talyn Kestrel and his family, allowed him to take control. Well, that wasn't exactly true. Gregory of Fal Carrach and Sarelle of Benewyn had vigorously protested his selection. They had been in the minority, though, and a good thing too.

The High King had given him two charges: exterminate the Marchers and extract from the Highland mines as much wealth as he possibly could. Killeran had learned quickly that the former was virtually impossible because of the tenacity of these uncivilized barbarians. The latter was working out quite well, however.

The mines located within the foothills had proven to be spectacularly profitable, for both the High King and himself. Rodric certainly didn't expect him to keep his hand out of the pot, did he? Especially when his hand was tied to that bastard Dinnegan. A worry for another day, though. The spoils that he had taken for himself had made him a wealthy man, and even more greedy. That was now one of the problems.

He had used captured Highlanders as his miners, working them until they died. Whether it was a man, woman or child didn't matter to him. All he cared about was how much they produced. Unfortunately, his methods were beginning to work against him. As a result, finding it more of a challenge to enslave Highlanders, he had sent his reivers into Dunmoor and the Clanwar Desert on occasion in search of new workers, but without much luck.

Most of the mines were in the same general location, so Killeran had built a fort in a strategic location that now served as his point of command. After seven years, though, the lowland mines were beginning to run dry. Consequently, he had found himself out in the cursed Highlands, leading his men on raids into the higher passes and valleys hunting for new workers and new veins. Even if Killeran could only work a mine for a few days before the Marchers disrupted his activities and forced his men back into the foothills, what he could gain from those few days exceeded months of labor at the lower elevations.

To remedy the situation, and to exert greater influence on the Marchers, he had requested assistance from the High King. Rodric had been less than happy to provide it, but did so nonetheless. Killeran's men were no match for the Marchers. That had been proven time and time again. The Marchers, however, were no match for the warlocks Rodric had given him.

Just thinking about those shadowspawn made his blood run cold. He had heard of sorcerers before, but thought they were relics of the past; of a time when the power of nature was much more than it was now; of a time when evil had not yet been discovered. Every time he thought about it, Killeran found the whole idea slightly preposterous. Where there was man there was evil. That was a simple truth.

The handful of warlocks Killeran took with him this morning made him wonder if the gold and silver he was stealing from the Highlands was worth it. Though he commanded them, he knew it was only because Rodric had ordered it. The power they controlled was immense, and worst of all, Killeran had no concept of where it came from or its limits, or perhaps Rodric did and just didn't care.

He didn't like it when he didn't know something. It made him uncomfortable, and nervous. It was difficult to tell the sorcerers apart, as they all wore dark, black robes with their hoods up, even on a warm day. The temperature, whether hot or cold, didn't seem to affect them. Killeran found that to be particularly alarming. Their only visible feature most of the time was their eyes, which were cold and black.

Those eyes had been human once, but no more. Perhaps it was the lack of humanity that unsettled him. It was rumored that the warlocks received their dark powers from the Shadow Lord himself. Glancing at them as they stood off to the side and slightly behind him, he decided that was one rumor he didn't need proven.

Nevertheless, it was because of them that his raiding parties were becoming more effective. The Marchers had no sorcerers of their own, and therefore no way to fight back. Finding new workers was simply a matter of locating the Highlanders' current hiding places. At least the warlocks served a purpose — making his life easier.

Killeran lowered his spyglass, rubbing his eye with his hand. Rising from his place on top of a small crest, he wiped off several spots of dirt from his gleaming silver breastplate before turning around. It was early morning, and the sky to the east slowly turned a dusky red.

He had just finished positioning his men for the morning's raid, though it did not look to be particularly promising. He had counted only a dozen small huts hidden among the trees below the ridge. He needed new workers desperately, but he doubted he would find many this morning. Still, he would take what he could get.

After the warlocks had eliminated the dogs, the Highlanders' first defense, they had captured the three sentries guarding the village. The Marchers had no chance against the power of the warlocks. In fact, this morning's raid, if all went as planned, would be more like a cattle roundup. With his men surrounding the small hamlet, their primary task was to make sure that no one escaped. Other than that they had little to do. The warlocks would do the rest, using their black arts to render the opposition unconscious.

He had taken him several hours to explain to the warlocks that a dead worker was a useless worker, but he had finally gotten it through to them. Now, rather than blowing a Highlander apart with a bolt of energy, they had refined their technique somewhat. By the time the Highlanders awoke, they would be in chains. All in all, Killeran thought it was a rather ingenious system, both efficient and ruthless.

Killeran brought the spyglass up again and surveyed the soon-to-be battlefield below him one more time. There was no reason for his men to hide. He wanted them to be seen. It would encourage the Highlanders to escape, and the only direction that was free of his reivers' presence led directly to his warlocks. He grinned in spite of his cold, not realizing that as his cheeks rose up, his resemblance to a rat became even more pronounced because of his long nose.

"You know what to do?" asked Killeran in a high-pitched voice.

Kursool and his other sergeants, standing behind him and well away from the warlocks, answered in unison. "Yes, milord."

"Good, then be about it. We have little time to waste. The warlocks have discovered two more villages within a day's ride of here. I mean to have them as well by the end of the day."

"Yes, milord." His three sergeants, all hardened veterans, ran off to their posts, each one in charge of a different compass point.

He, too, would have preferred to be away from the warlocks.

Though they appeared to be less than human, they did retain certain human desires. He had heard the screams of women coming from their barracks many times. Bloodcurdling screams. Screams of despair. He had never gone to investigate, afraid of what he might discover. The remains of the women that were found one morning had sickened him. Those that still lived looked as if their companions, the ones who had not survived the night, were the lucky ones.

Killeran tore his mind away from his dark thoughts. The attack would begin in fifteen minutes, in plenty of time to retain a measure of surprise. Full light was still an hour away. Killeran tried to wait calmly, though his agitation only increased as each second passed.

A letter from the High King had arrived just a few days before, demanding to know why the shipment of gold from the Highlands had dwindled to almost nothing. He'd have to think of a good reason for that. Maybe he could blame the High-landers, and say that they had intercepted several of the wagon trains. Yes, that might be the way to do it. Then Rodric might be persuaded to send him even more men.

The High King had been reluctant so far, worried that the other Kingdoms would notice and question his motives. But if Killeran had more men, he'd have a much easier time forcing his way into the higher passes. If he could win the higher passes, the wealth he could reap from the mines there would double, perhaps even triple his monthly output. Yes, that was an excellent idea. Motioning to the warlocks behind him, he began making his way down the crest.

18

LEARNING HIS TRADE

The smell of cinnamon rolls baking in the oven forced Thomas' eyes open. The morning sunshine was just beginning to push its way through the window. Rising from his bed, he leaned on the windowsill and looked out into the Shadowwood. A promising day. A clear sky, if a bit chilly. Thomas walked over to the washstand and splashed water left from the night before on his face and brushed his teeth with soda. After pulling on a new shirt, a relatively clean pair of breeks and his boots, he grabbed his cloak and the pack he had prepared the night before, then headed down the stairs.

He remembered quite vividly the first time he had gone across to the Highlands on his own. It happened almost a year before, soon after he had joined the Sylvana. Rya hadn't liked that at all, and he could even recall her exact words.

"You think you're going across by yourself?" The surprise in her voice set off a chord within him.

"Why can't I?" he replied. "The Highlands are my responsibility."

Rya didn't respond. She couldn't think of a valid argument,

and Thomas knew it. That didn't keep her from trying to do what she thought was best, though.

"Fine," she said. "But Rynlin is going with you."

Up until then, Rynlin had sat calmly at the kitchen table, eating his breakfast and trying not to draw any attention to himself. Now, he had been caught in the middle of a war of wills. He had looked from Rya's fiery eyes to Thomas' flashing with anger, and once again knew that regardless of what he said, he was going to get himself into trouble.

"Thomas will have to go across on his own. I've got too many things to do today as it is."

He had then buried himself in his meal. Rya's shock at his response was clear as her eyes threatened to pop out of her head. Seeing his opportunity, Thomas quickly gathered his things and left the house before Rya could berate her husband into changing his mind.

That day had turned out to be more exciting than he had ever expected. No sooner had he set foot in the Highlands when a feeling of evil drew him off to the west. He had never forgotten the sense of darkness that came from the Nightstalker, but this was a sharper, unfamiliar feeling. Nevertheless, it was not to be confused with any other. Dark creatures wandered the Highlands. His Highlands. As a Sylvan Warrior, keeping his homeland free of the Shadow Lord's minions was his responsibility. He tracked the evil for most of the morning, finally finding the source some two or three leagues from where he landed on the coast.

A pack of Fearhounds had attacked a small farmhouse hidden away in a valley, most likely built there to avoid Killeran's reivers. Unfortunately, it wasn't very well protected, and the farmer's closest neighbor lived several miles away. The farmer had gotten his family inside before the Fearhounds attacked. Despite their repeated attempts the Fearhounds couldn't break in because of the stone walls and stout wood doors, so they had taken up residence in the yard.

Moving on silent feet through the surrounding forest, Thomas climbed a small hill rising above the farmhouse. The huge dogs were oblivious to everything around them except their selected prey. After scanning the area to ensure that there were no other dangers to worry about, he pulled several arrows from his quiver. He shot three Fearhounds before the beasts even realized they were under attack. By the time they discovered from which direction, six lay dead in the short grass with arrows through the eye.

Thomas had been very careful with his shooting. The only sure way to kill a Fearhound because of their thick almost armored hide was with an arrow through the eye. They could shrug off any other blow. The remaining three made a futile charge up the hill, never thinking to circle around and come through the trees, which would have made it more difficult for Thomas to get a clear shot. Most sane men ran at the sight of a single Fearhound, much less stood their ground against three. But Thomas' feet were rooted to the soil. So caught up in his task, the thought of fleeing never crossed his mind.

He had marveled at their size and speed. Fearhound, in his opinion, was a misnomer. There was no mistaking their resemblance to normal hounds in terms of the shape of their bodies, but they were actually the size of small ponies, their top two canine teeth extending beyond their lower jaw. Thomas targeted the largest Fearhounds in the pack first. He did so again as the three beasts attacked.

Two of the charging Fearhounds died before they reached the base of the hill. Thomas let the third get a little closer. He had done well so far, and he didn't want to make a mistake. The snarl, the sharp teeth, the saliva dripping from the mouth of the enraged Fearhound heightened his anticipation, his adrenaline from the skirmish coursing though his veins.

He focused solely on his target — the eye. Sighting carefully, he took a deep breath, then released the bowstring. The arrow flew true to its mark, taking the last Fearhound in the eye and knocking it back down the hill.

The whole skirmish lasted no more than a minute or two. Yet, by the end of it, Thomas was sweating profusely. It was then that he realized exactly what he had accomplished. If Rya found out about what he had just done, she'd do much worse to him than the Fearhounds ever could. When his body started to shake he decided it was time to go. The farmer would have to clean up the mess himself.

When had he stopped thinking? The better question was when had he completely lost his senses? Only a fool would stand calmly on a hill and shoot arrows at a pack of Fearhounds, so certain of his skill that he knew he could kill all nine. But he had done it, without even considering the Talent as a possible weapon. He hadn't wanted to waste his strength.

The shakes left him a few hours later, replaced by a feeling of satisfaction. Thomas had known since his time on the Stone that his true enemy was the Shadow Lord. Though he could not get at him directly, he could hurt him in other ways. Every one of the Shadow Lord's creatures that Thomas destroyed was another prick in the skin of the Shadow Lord, and a miniscule weakening of his power. A more noble cause Thomas could not imagine.

From that point forward, Thomas took every opportunity to cross into the Highlands. Yet, his desire to go there came only in part from the fact that the Highlands was his responsibility, as decreed by the Sylvana. Rather, he was still unsure of how to handle the burden placed on him by Talyn.

This was his land, and his people, but what could one person do? What could he do? And would the Highlanders really want to see him?

They had never really considered him one of their own,

viewing him as an outsider and a freak, in some respects, because of his mother's abilities. Because of his uncertainty, instead he tried to help his people when he could in his own way. Though his guilt remained, his constant forays across the channel lessened it somewhat.

Thomas walked into the kitchen and greeted his grandparents, who sat at the table finishing their breakfasts. Rya's eyebrows rose in a questioning glance upon seeing Thomas set his weapons and an extra quiver of arrows by the door, her face twisting with concern. Thomas ignored her and scooped out a helping of porridge, sprinkled some sugar on top, settled into a chair and dug in hungrily.

Rya didn't like her grandson's more and more frequent excursions to the Highlands, but she couldn't stop him. Though Thomas was a Sylvan Warrior, and the Highlands were his to protect, that didn't stop her from worrying. Of course, Rynlin showed little concern for the actions of his grandson, which irritated her to no end. She felt like she had to do the worrying for the both of them.

"So where are you off to this morning?" she asked, already knowing the answer.

"To the Highlands."

"Of course, the Highlands. You certainly do have a good day for it." No matter how hard she tried, small flecks of worry crept into her voice.

"Have you heard of this Raptor?" asked Rynlin, jumping into the conversation. "This person, or creature perhaps, is developing quite a reputation."

Thomas almost leapt out of his seat upon hearing the name, but he controlled the reflex, just barely. Keeping his eyes averted, he focused on eating the rest of his porridge.

"No, no I haven't," said Rya. Maybe her husband was worried after all.

"Well, it's supposedly a man or creature of some sort," said

Rynlin, leaning forward in his chair so that he was directly across from Thomas. Thomas tried to ignore Rynlin, but it was hard to do when his grandfather hovered over his breakfast. "The few people who live in the Burren and Oakwood Forest, as well as many Highlanders, have sworn they've seen it, whatever it may be. It's even been seen near the Breaker. Anyway, almost every time Ogren or Shades or Fearhounds are sighted in the region, this Raptor shows up as well. People say this Raptor fought a Shade and tore it apart limb by limb."

Rynlin sat back in his chair, giving Thomas some room, but his eyes retained their questioning gaze. "Personally, I think it must be a man. You need hands if you're going to use a bow, and that seems to be one of its preferred weapons. Are you sure you haven't heard any of these stories, Thomas?"

"A few perhaps," he replied, scooping the last of the porridge into his mouth. He hoped that his expression was one of innocence. Unfortunately, he didn't think he was fooling anyone.

The slow speed of Rynlin's investigation wore on Rya's nerves, so she took over for her husband. "Rynlin, you always take so long to get to the point." She turned her steely eyes on Thomas. "You're getting quite a reputation, Thomas."

"Maybe," he said noncommittally. At times he could be remarkably mature. At others, much to his grandmother's annoyance, he could act like a child. "It really wasn't something I was looking for. I'm just doing what I'm supposed to be doing as a member of the Sylvana."

"You are, Thomas," said Rynlin. "But you don't have to rid the Highlands of every single dark creature all by yourself."

"I assume you're being careful?"

"Rya, after everything you and Rynlin taught me, don't you think I can take care of myself?"

"We don't doubt your skills, Thomas," said Rynlin. "We just don't want you to get overconfident."

"Don't worry. I won't."

Swinging his legs out from underneath the table, Thomas slung his pack over his shoulder with his bow and extra quiver of arrows. After adjusting the sword at his hip, he made his way to the oven and grabbed a few cinnamon rolls cooling on the windowsill before heading for the door. On his way out, he gave his grandmother a kiss on the cheek. He had learned a long time before that killing someone with kindness, especially someone as irascible as his grandmother, was often the best course of action.

"You're insufferable," she called after him as he walked out the door, laughing under her breath.

"I know," he replied as he closed the door behind him. The Highlands were beckoning.

Rya sighed. "I worry about him."

"I know. But this is what he is now, for a while longer anyway. Besides, I think it helps him in a way."

"Putting himself in danger all the time?" Rynlin ignored his wife's sarcastic tone. Sometimes she let her concern get the better of her, and it usually came out through her vitriolic tongue.

"No," replied Rynlin, refusing to be baited. He didn't feel like arguing with his wife this morning. "What I mean is, if your family was murdered, or rather the one person you cared about most as a child, and you knew who was ultimately responsible, and you now had a way to get back at him, wouldn't you take every opportunity to do so?"

Rya thought about it for a moment, but Rynlin already knew her answer. "Yes, I guess I would."

Rynlin sat back in his chair, extending his legs underneath the table, a satisfied smile on his face.

"But that's not really what's bothering me," said Rya. Rynlin knew it immediately. It was going to be one of those mornings. Mornings he had come to dread over the years.

"What are you worried about?"

"When Thomas is off the island, he can be found." All of Rya's fears were coming to the surface, and her voice grew louder as a result. "The Shadow Lord knows who he is now. We knew that as soon as he stood on the Stone. He could send a Nightstalker after him again. If he's too far into the Highlands, we wouldn't be able to help him in time."

"Well, that is a valid concern," said Rynlin.

"Thank you very much for agreeing."

Based on the sharpness of her tone, the vitriol was virtually spilling from her. Rynlin sighed. It was going to be a wonderful day. And the morning had gotten off to such an excellent start. He kept the sarcasm to himself, of course. No need to irritate his wife further. When he was younger he might have voiced his thought, but that would have only pushed Rya closer to the edge. He was thankful that he had gotten somewhat wiser with age.

"Rya, I don't think we have to worry about that, at least for the time being."

"And why not?"

"Because all of the Shadow Lord's previous attempts have failed, and Thomas is much stronger now. If a Nightstalker comes within a league of him, Thomas will know. And if that happens, I'd be more worried for the Nightstalker." Rynlin's attempt at humor only made Rya's face turn sourer, so he continued. "Besides, if the Shadow Lord really wants to find him, whether or not Thomas is on the Isle of Mist won't matter. There is no place Thomas can hide from him. All we can do is let him live his life and hope that he listened to some of what we tried to teach him."

Rya let out a long breath and relaxed into the back of her chair. "I know you're right, Rynlin, but I still don't like it."

"I don't like it either," said Rynlin. "Now why don't you bring over a few of those cinnamon rolls. They smell delicious."

The look Rya gave him could have burned through steel. "If you want one, get it yourself. I might be your wife, but I'm not your servant."

Rynlin sighed inwardly. The conversation had been going so well. Rynlin decided that he was going to have to pay more attention to Rya's moods today. Otherwise he was going to get himself into more trouble than usual, and that was quite a lot as it was.

19

———

ATTACKED

Oso had lain in bed for most of the night, unable to sleep. He certainly should have. His body demanded it, but his mind won out. He had spent the past week clearing a small patch of burned-out forest to increase the size of the village's fields for next spring's planting.

Now finished, he could take some time for himself — and go hunting. Unfortunately, the excitement of the day to come had worked against him during the night. As the hours slowly passed he had considered getting an early start just after midnight. Reason had won out, though, and he decided to leave at first light.

Like most Highlanders, hunting was one of his passions. The challenge of the chase never failed to get his adrenaline flowing. Nevertheless, his desire to hunt was stronger than usual. Though he would never admit it to anyone other than himself, he really just wanted to escape the village for a time. Lately, people had been treating him differently, and it was making him extremely uncomfortable. He would much rather confront a charging boar than deal with the looks some of the village women directed toward him.

Oso's father died soon after the Crag fell, and his mother a few years after, a victim of the mines. Oso shifted on his bed — a few blocks of wood, a large board and an old straw mattress with more holes than cloth — and set his feet on the dirt floor of his hut. He ran his large hands through his long, blond hair in frustration. He had wanted to save his mother, but couldn't. No one could have. Not with Killeran's warlocks about.

Even still, his failure haunted him almost every day. Though no one ever mentioned it, they all knew why he trained so hard during his weapons practice. Only one person could best him now in the circle — Alus — and that wouldn't last for much longer. Thinking of what had happened to his family, even now, years past, still made his blood boil.

Since then, the women of his village had looked after him. Oso politely turned down several offers to move into their homes. He didn't want to burden anyone. Instead, he built his own, small hut at the very edge of the village. Of course, he was not above allowing the women to mend his shirts or make him a new pair of pants when needed. There were certain things he just didn't have the skill or the patience for. Because of his circumstances, all the village women saw him as their own. Now, he sensed they saw him as something else. The change occurred when he reached his seventeenth summer just a month before.

Now, the women always seemed to weigh him with their eyes, and several, the ones with daughters, had taken a particular interest in him. What made him even more uncomfortable, though, were the daughters. Oso was a shy boy, and the suggestive looks and teasing he received from the girls set his face on fire. Those who succeeded in making him blush laughed in delight. Even worse, his embarrassment only made them intensify their efforts. After what Sara had said the day before, his need to get away increased. Her daughter, Kera, really was quite beautiful, and Oso liked the way her black curls drifted over her eyes when she bent her head. But there was something in those eyes that worried him.

"You're a man now," she had said. Oso remembered the words exactly, and they had played through his mind a dozen times during the night. "My Kera really is quite a catch, Kylin. Perhaps you'd like to join us for dinner on the morrow?"

It was a seemingly innocuous conversation. Normally, it would not have bothered him. But she had called him Kylin! His given name. Hearing it set off a warning bell in his head. She had called him Kylin! Many Highland children grew up with nicknames. When the adults decided to use your proper name, it meant that you were ready to marry. For the last month he had laughed off the hints thrown his way, not taking them seriously. But now, what was he to do? If he wasn't careful, within the week he could be betrothed. And the week after that married! He wasn't ready for that.

"Women," he mumbled to himself in frustration.

Oso rose to his feet, his head just inches from the ceiling. His broad shoulders and large frame filled the small hut completely. Running his hand over his jaw, he decided the few soft whiskers there could wait. If he left now, he could escape the village without anyone knowing. Then he wouldn't open his door like he had a few days before in his underclothes to find Rea and her daughter there with a basket of bread and fruit. No, he certainly didn't want to repeat that experience. Both Rea and Lisel had found the whole episode remarkably amusing, particularly when they discovered that his blushing affected more than just his face.

After pulling a somewhat clean white shirt over his head, he tucked it into his green breeks. He then dug around in a small pile of dirty clothes to find the dark brown jacket he wanted. It had gotten cold fast this year. He guessed it would be a very short autumn. Slipping the jacket over his shoulders, he realized that some of the tiny rips across the back weren't so tiny anymore. He'd need a new jacket soon. If only he knew how to sew! Then he could avoid any more potential embarrassments. Well, there was nothing he could do about it now. Oso turned to his small table and threw a leftover crust of bread and some apples into his travel sack. Slinging his bow and a quiver of arrows over his shoulder, he grabbed his sword with his free hand.

He opened the small door of his home quietly and was just as careful as he let it fall back in place as he stepped outside. There was no reason to wake everybody, now was there? The sun was rising in the east, setting the clouds on the horizon awash in red. Within the hour others in his village would stir. Oso spun around in surprise at the soft snap of a twig behind him. No one would be up and about this early. Why would someone—

Reivers! Reivers in the village! Their familiar black leather armor was burned into his memory. Two had just walked right past his home, intent on the cottages in front of them. Many of his fellow Highlanders had laughed at his house when he had finished. His hut resembled a small, stunted tree rather than a cottage and blended quite well with the forest. Now Oso thanked his lack of skill in carpentry for allowing the reivers to mistake it for a tree.

Oso silently put down his travel sack and shrugged the bow and quiver from his shoulder. His sword was out of its sheath and in the back of one of the reivers before he had time to think. The sound of the reiver sliding off of Oso's blade made the other reiver turn, but the raider was too slow. He was greeted by the slash of Oso's sword across his throat. The man clutched at the blood pouring from his neck, falling to the ground with his life seeping into the soil. The entire struggle took only a few seconds. Exhilaration rushed through Oso. Finally he could get back at the men responsible for the deaths of his parents. All the hours and days and years of training were worth it, just for those two kills.

Oso quickly came to his senses. He didn't have time to exult in his success. The battle had not even begun. At least a hundred or more reivers moved toward the center of the village in a large inverted skirmish line, which meant there were probably warlocks at the far end. He didn't have a moment to lose. He ran toward the village green shouting at the top of his lungs.

"Reivers! Reivers in the village! Rise and fight!"

He made it only a few feet before he met two more reivers, this time without the benefit of surprise. Oso skidded to a halt, barely avoiding an extended sword. He swung down with his own sword with all his strength, knocking the man's blade from his hand. A quick kick to the black-clad soldier's midsection sent him reeling to the ground with broken ribs.

Oso turned his attention to the other reiver, who carried a two-headed axe. The soldier swung a vicious downstroke, which would have left Oso without his head if the blow connected. Ducking underneath the assault, Oso stabbed at the reiver's gut, but his opponent recovered quickly and blocked the thrust. The man moved back a few steps to gain room to maneuver. Oso decided now was the time to even the odds. It was not something he relished doing, but was necessary.

Jumping back a few steps, Oso stabbed backwards with his sword, keeping his eyes on the reiver in front of him. The man with the broken ribs had been trying to get up, and Oso couldn't take a chance on an attack from behind. His broken ribs were now the least of the dying man's concerns.

The ruthlessness of Oso's action registered in the other reiver's eyes. As the raider nervously shifted his grip on the axe, Oso charged forward, taking advantage of the man's indecision. Caught by surprise, the reiver blocked the sword stroke Oso aimed toward his head with the hilt of his axe, but was too slow when Oso swung back across his body, slicing open the man's stomach. The soldier fell to his knees, screaming in pain as his guts poured out on the soft earth.

Turning his attention back to the village, Oso breathed a sigh of relief. His warning had not gone unheeded. The Highlanders had burst from their cottages with a vengeance, swords and spears at the ready, and formed a circle of steel around a few central cottages. Expecting an easy victory, the reivers nearly broke against the ferocity of the Highlanders' defense, but their numbers bolstered them and their line held.

20

ESCAPE

Killeran had walked halfway down the ridge when he heard the warning shout from just outside the village. He stopped abruptly, a look of disgust on his face. Someone had made a mistake, and when he found out who, he'd make sure the bastard never made another mistake ever again. He should have known. This small raid was already more trouble than it was worth.

He wiped his nose on his damp sleeve yet again. This blasted cold! If he wasn't in these cursed mountains, he wouldn't have to blow his nose every other minute. The Highlanders had rushed from their homes like caged mountain lions newly freed. His reivers stood little chance against them. Now his only hope for success lay with his warlocks, who marched along behind him. The thought made him shiver. He liked to know exactly where his warlocks were every second, but he preferred to have them as far from himself as possible. Nevertheless, they would be the key to his victory today.

The Highlanders had driven his men back and formed a defensive ring around three houses in the center of the village. Why would they do that? He had expected them to try to fight their way free. If they broke through his reivers, they would be almost impossible to catch in the forest.

Wait! The women and children! None had emerged from the huts. That must be why! If they were still in those cottages, his plan might still work. Highlanders would rather die in battle than surrender to the mines, and they would never abandon their women and children. He just needed to get his warlocks closer. Killeran ran down the steep slope, desperate to salvage something from this ill-starred raid.

21

———

TAKING CHARGE

The reivers had formed their own, larger ring around that of the Highlanders. Not expecting an attack from behind, Oso took full advantage of that fact, stabbing two in the lower back before leaping across the space between the two steel rings to stand with his people. The histories said not fighting someone face to face, as a man should, was the mark of a coward. Oso had learned quickly that real life differed greatly from what was written in a book. In a battle you fought to survive. However you accomplished your task didn't really matter, as long as you were still standing when the sun set.

His sword covered in red, Oso was thankful that the spots of blood on his shirt were not his own. This certainly wasn't the way he had hoped his day would begin.

"What happened to the guards?" he asked a tall Highlander, long blond hair matted to his face by a mixture of sweat and blood. One of the reiver's had gotten lucky and opened a small gash across the Highlander's forehead.

"Taken by the warlocks probably," grunted Alus, as he ran through a reiver who got too close to his long reach. Alus then caught on his sword the blade of another reiver who tried to take him unawares. With lightning speed Alus reversed his movement, bringing his gleaming blade up in a wide arc. The steel caught the reiver on the side of the head, slicing it open.

On an order by one of the sergeants, the reivers disengaged. They had lost a dozen men, with several more seriously wounded, trying to break through the Highlanders' defensive shell. The sergeant decided that was enough for now.

"You did well, Oso," said Alus, stepping back from the fray for a moment. The Highlanders alongside him quickly shifted the ring to compensate for the missing blade in their moving wall of steel. "If you hadn't warned us, we wouldn't have stood a chance. They would have caught us in our beds."

"Luck, I guess," said Oso, looking to the ground and shrugging his broad shoulders. Oso felt incredibly uncomfortable when under the gaze of a beautiful girl. He felt only slightly less so when praised for his efforts.

"Luck or no, you acted rightly." Alus clapped him on the back with pride. "You know what to do?" The Highlanders remained in their defensive circle, their eyes watching the enemy around them with wary eyes.

"Yes."

Alus scanned the reivers around them, then the forest just beyond. He was looking for something specific, but he hadn't found it yet. "Then be about it. We can stand against the reivers. Once the warlocks attack we won't last very long. Can you make it in thirty minutes?"

Oso nodded reluctantly. He wanted to stand and fight, his blood rushing through his veins, his senses heightened. He felt more alive than he ever had before. No one in the village could best him except for Alus, and he had proven the truth of that just now, having already eliminated four reivers. He was a Highlander, and would have been a Marcher if the Highland Lord had not been murdered those many years before. Oso kept his thoughts to himself, though. He knew what he had to do. Alus had given him this task as a sign of respect for his maturity. Though he had been a boy then, and was now a man, the task remained his to accomplish. He would do what was needed.

"Then you have thirty minutes."

Oso didn't bother to acknowledge Alus. He had a job to do, and there was no time to waste. Running into the nearest cottage, he pulled the door closed behind him, then locked it. A large table with two benches running alongside it stood by the fireplace. Thankfully, nothing sat on its top.

Careful not to disturb the benches, Oso went to the corner of the table facing north, then pressed with his foot on the wood floor board running perpendicular to the table leg. The table silently rose upwards, its legs still attached to the floor that came up with it. A pitch-black hole greeted him when he knelt down to look beneath the floor. So far so good. He resheathed his sword. He'd have to wipe the steel clean later.

Though he couldn't see a ladder, he knew one was there. If anyone but a Highlander discovered the opening, they would be hard-pressed to find a way down without a length of rope. The Highlanders had built the ladder into the side of the tunnel. Because of that, you had to know the position of the rungs. Otherwise, you'd drop forty feet before landing on the stone floor. Swinging his legs into the darkness, he felt for the first ladder rung with his foot. Catching it with his toes, he started down.

He had never remembered the escape tunnel being so cramped before, his shoulders scraping against the sides. He didn't have time to be careful, though. Alus had given him thirty minutes, and that's all he'd get. Halfway down the hole, Oso pushed in a knob he found with his hand next to the ladder rung. The hatch, table and all, closed, shutting him in complete darkness. He'd have to move by memory now. A few seconds later his feet touched the ground. He waited for his eyes to adjust to the darkness before continuing.

As he walked through the tunnel, he hunched over slightly to avoid the low ceiling. He saw the basic outline of the roughly cut rock walls, but little else, which forced him to go slower than he wanted. He traveled through the tunnel a few minutes longer, trailing his hand along the wall, when the glimmer of a torch appeared before him in the distance.

"Hold," whispered a harsh voice. Oso felt the steel pressed against his stomach. One jab and he'd have the luxury of a slow and painful death.

"After spending so much time baking bread and treats for me, Lara, do you want to ruin it all by gutting me like a fish?"

"No, Oso," her sigh of relief audible. "Can't afford to take any chances, though."

Lara resheathed the dagger and led him down the tunnel toward the light.

"Are the men holding?" she asked anxiously.

"For now," replied Oso. "We only have twenty minutes. Warlocks."

Lara grunted her understanding. "Then let's be about it."

When they reached the end of the tunnel, Lara pulled the torch from the sconce in the stone and pushed in on an irregularly shaped stone. The wall in front of her slid quietly to the side. Stepping out into a small ravine a half-mile from the village, Oso shielded his eyes for a moment from the bright sun.

He was glad to see that all of the women and children had made it out of the village. The younger children, many only a few years old, clung in fear to their mothers' skirts. They didn't know what was going on. That was for the best, probably. The older children knew exactly what had happened, and though they were afraid, they retained their composure. Nonetheless, they remained close to their mothers. The women were afraid too, but that was barely noticeable through their looks of determination. If not for the children, the women would have joined the men. Most of the stories spoke about the skill of the Marchers, yet the Highland women received the same training as the men. Gender meant little to the Highlanders. Only a person's abilities mattered.

As Oso gazed at the women and children, he realized that their eyes had turned to him. He was the leader now.

"Is everyone accounted for?"

"Yes, Oso," answered Rea, her daughter Lisel standing next to her. He was supposed to have dinner with them later in the week. When Lisel had asked, he didn't know how to say no, but the thought of being stuck between the two as they teased him mercilessly about settling down and finding a wife had set his stomach on edge. Now, the thought of dinner with the two sounded quite appealing.

"All right, then." Oso filled his voice with a sternness that sounded foreign to his ears, yet he hoped it gave his charges a feeling of confidence. "Let's not allow the efforts of Alus and the others go to waste. We have twenty minutes. Everyone knows what to do. Lara, please shut the tunnel door."

Wordlessly Lara walked back to the opening in the ravine wall. She pressed in on a portion of the stone that looked no different than any other and the door swung shut soundlessly.

"Thank you. Lara, you stay in the rear. If you see any sign of pursuit, give a yell. Now remember, if we are attacked, scatter. Go to ground then head for the higher passes. Is that understood?"

He waited until everyone nodded. The fear that battled with determination in the eyes of many of the women, even some of the older children, disappeared. Oso had given them a task, a purpose, and they would focus on that. They would forget their fears and their worries — for now.

"Good. Single file, mothers carrying small children. Let's go."

Oso moved to the front and the Highlanders hastened to obey his commands, the women picking up any small children who could not keep up, the older children forming a line. As he led the motley band out through the ravine and into the forest, he wondered if they would make it. They had a long way to go until they reached the safety of the higher passes. He hoped Alus bought them enough time to escape. They would need every second of it.

22

—————

PLAN GONE AWRY

Those fools! He had given specific orders, but they had failed to follow them. Those stupid fools! He had told them not to engage the Highlanders, just keep them in the same place long enough for the warlocks to arrive. The warlocks needed room to work their Dark Magic. If the reivers were too close, then they would be affected by it as well. But no, as soon as the shout of warning had been given, the sergeants had ordered their men to attack. And now, when the sergeants finally gave the order to disengage and form a circle around the Highlanders, they hadn't moved back far enough. The fools!

Killeran finally reached the bottom of the crest and entered the trees leading to the village. He motioned with his hand, and one of the warlocks stepped forward. He found the warlock's gaze unnerving. Most people betrayed some emotion with their eyes, whether fear or pain or hate. The eyes of a warlock betrayed nothing. They were empty, devoid of emotion, which made them all the more unpredictable. Killeran equated that unpredictability with danger.

"Yes, milord?"

The grating voice set Killeran's teeth on edge. It sounded

metallic rather than human. "Take your men around to the east, over there, by that gap in the trees. You can approach from that direction."

"Yes, milord." The warlock stepped back and motioned for his companions to follow. At least Killeran didn't have to worry about the warlocks obeying his commands.

As Killeran broke through the trees, he saw that his sergeants had finally realized their mistake and were pulling their men farther back in anticipation of the warlocks' arrival. Seeing him approach, the three sergeants ran over to report. He didn't pay any attention, though, as they babbled on like children. He had seen everything that had happened with his own eyes. A quick slash of his hand through the air shut them up. Many generals said that you needed the respect of your men to lead them effectively. Killeran disagreed. In his opinion, you needed their fear, and he had captured that long before.

As he studied the situation, something nagged at him. A boy had run into one of the houses just a few minutes before. Killeran had assumed that he had gone looking for a bow, but the boy had not yet emerged from the dwelling. That was odd. The Highlanders seemed quite content to wait there, in their loose circle around the three houses, for him to make the next move. They could obviously see the warlocks moving around them now, but they didn't seem to care. The boy. What could the boy be up—

Tunnels! That had to be it. The Highlanders hadn't remained to protect the women and children. Instead, they wanted to buy time for their escape.

"Kursool, move the men forward from the west. Push the Highlanders toward that gap in the trees. Now!"

Kursool jumped into motion, startled by Killeran's sharp command. He quickly obeyed, yelling orders to the reivers.

Grabbing another sergeant by the arm, Killeran yelled shrilly into his face. "Help him! Get those men moving now!"

As the second sergeant ran after the first, Killeran turned his attention back to the Highlanders. A tall Highlander was giving orders now, making sure that all of his men heard his words. What was he telling them?

Before the sergeants could get their men moving, the Highlanders charged forward, their bloodcurdling yells echoing through the trees. The large Highlander had picked his spot carefully, looking for a weakness in the circle of reivers. It hadn't taken him long to find it. And just in time, too. The warlocks were almost in position.

The Highlanders ran forward, swinging their weapons above their heads, yelling at the top of their lungs. However, right before they charged into the northern side of reivers, the Highlanders reversed direction, running full speed to the south and catching the reivers behind them completely by surprise. Not expecting the attack, the reivers on that side barely had time to raise their weapons before the Highlanders struck.

At the same time, the reivers to the north stood there dumbstruck by the tactic, and many just a little thankful. None had any true desire to come face to face with a Highlander. In a matter of seconds, the Highlanders had broken through the reivers to the south, leaving a trail of dead black-clad raiders behind them. As they got deeper into the trees, the Highlanders scattered to further confuse the reivers, as well as draw them away from the women and children, now hopefully on their way into the higher passes.

The Highlanders' tactic surprised Killeran just as much as it did his men. He quickly recovered, however, cursing his men and doing his best to get them to regroup, but to no avail. The Highlanders had won their freedom, at least for a time. Killeran had planned everything so perfectly, and now it was a disaster.

"So much for those other villages," he muttered under his breath.

He'd be lucky to come away with a handful of new workers

now, and he was already counting the three sentries he had captured with the warlocks' aid before the raid even began. He would have preferred to capture the Marchers since they lasted longer in the mines, but pursuing them would be a waste of time. No, maybe he could salvage something from this mess after all. Women and children never lived as long as the men in the mines, but they could still work there, for a time.

23

A NEW PATH

Every time Thomas entered the Highlands, a surge of adrenaline rushed through his body. This time he started in the southeast and traveled along the Fal Carrachian border for several days. Lately, each of his visits to the Highlands brought him in contact with Ogren or Shades, and even a few Fearhounds. The Shadow Lord's minions preferred roaming the northern border because of its proximity to the Northern Steppes. During the last few months, though, the Shadow Lord's spawn had hunted farther and farther south. Thomas found that particularly odd, but had no answer for it. Neither did Rynlin, who normally had an answer for everything. Hence his decision to search in the south first.

As he wandered through the lush forest, gazed at breathtaking peaks and passed hidden mountain lakes, a sense of anticipation filled him. Fighting the creatures of the Shadow Lord gave him a particular pleasure, or rather a feeling of completeness, as if he was doing what he was meant to do. The last time he came this far south he ran across a squad of Ogren. Beluil accompanied him then and they spent the better part of the day stalking the beasts. When evening approached, the five Ogren settled in for the night in a small gully.

Thomas and Beluil waited until the moon moved well across the sky before making their move. It was simple, really, as he silently stepped among the large, dark shapes and Beluil stood guard, watching for any sudden movements. Using his dagger, Thomas slit their throats with nary a sound. It wasn't the most honorable form of combat, but it was effective. Thomas had learned long before that when you drew steel, you fought to survive. How you accomplished that really didn't matter, as long as you lived to fight another day.

He had just eliminated the last Ogren when Beluil growled softly. Out of the corner of his eye, he noticed a shadow gliding along the edge of the gully. The moon dominated the sky that night and the wind remained still. None of the other shadows created by the branches and bushes that encroached on the gully stirred. Rising from his crouch, Thomas pretended to keep his attention on the final Ogren. A deep growl issued from Beluil's maw as the shadow came closer. Thomas communicated to his friend to stay quiet and still. Beluil obeyed, albeit reluctantly.

The evil emanating from the Ogren disappeared, but a new one replaced it and steadily grew stronger. The shadow crept closer. Sweat streaked down Thomas' face as he waited with his back turned. The feeling of evil increased as the shadow moved at a snail's pace along the edge of the gully. Thomas watched from the corner of his eye, but still he waited. Beluil wanted to strike, and the large wolf tensed, ready to launch himself at the approaching shadow. Thomas ordered him to wait. It was not an easy thing for a wolf to do.

The shadow continued to inch along the tree line, blending in with the darkness. At times, Thomas could just make it out. But he didn't have to see it to know where it was. The feeling of evil intensified as it ever so slowly glided closer. The muscles in

Thomas' hand itched to grasp his sword as the hairs on the back of his neck stood on end. He waited, though, ignoring the cold sweat running down his brow. The shadow drifted across the open space, approaching him from behind.

The blood pounded in Thomas' head, his mind screaming for him to do something — anything! He remained still, not yet making a move. The shadow was almost upon him, now no more than a few paces away. Just a little closer. Just one more step. In a single motion Thomas pulled his sword from its scabbard and whipped around, swinging the blade in a high, curving arc. A single moment of resistance jolted his arm before the blade continued smoothly on its course. The shadow crumpled at his feet. Beluil leaped forward, prepared to attack if Thomas had failed to strike true. The moonlight revealed an attacker dressed all in black with a black, steel sword in its hand.

A Shade. Thomas had sliced cleanly through its neck. The body convulsed a few times before finally lying still. Beluil watched it warily until he was certain that it no longer posed a threat. The head had landed a few paces away, coming to stand right side up. Thomas had seen only a handful of Shades in his lifetime and was glad for it. Deadly fighters, they reminded him of a snake. Their sinuous yet graceful movements could trick the eye, and a single touch from their swords meant death.

The taletellers said that Shades had once been men, but that the Shadow Lord had changed them with his Dark Magic. If they had once been human, there was no longer any sign of it. From a distance a Shade appeared as any other man, with long, dark hair and black clothes. Yet, their skin held a ghoulish cast. And their eyes always gave them away. Their milky white, soulless eyes. Thomas didn't sleep for two days after that encounter, his nerves still on edge. Where he found the fortitude to stand with his back turned to a Shade he didn't know.

Turning north a few days after entering the Highlands, and

then east once again to make his way back to the coast, Thomas decided that his normal prey had taken to ground, so he adjusted his sights. Whenever dark creatures absented themselves from the Highlands, Thomas instead spent his time hunting reivers. It was remarkable, really. These enemy soldiers occupied a land in which they had failed to conquer the inhabitants, yet they often wandered around as if it was their own, not recognizing the dangers presented by the Marchers and the terrain until it was too late.

His poor luck held, however. He normally found reivers in the foothills, but not this time. Disappointed, Thomas had almost made it back to the coast when he sensed Dark Magic to the west. He immediately went in that direction, moving from the foothills to the higher elevations. The darkness that clouded his senses every time he came in contact with Dark Magic originated several leagues away, and he knew the cause.

Warlocks, which meant a raiding party. But why would they risk searching for Marchers outside of the foothills? The higher passes still belonged to the Highlanders. Whoever made the decision to come this far took a huge risk, which meant Killeran was desperate. You couldn't run the mines without workers, and only his need for more explained this course of action.

The Dark Magic of the warlocks felt very much like the evil Thomas sensed when Ogren or Shades entered the Highlands, but this darkness was more twisted, and more subtle, as if some experiment had gone terribly wrong. He had only come face to face with a warlock once before, when he accompanied Rynlin on a trip to the Breaker. The feeling of wrongness that came from the warlock never left Thomas. Just thinking of the experience made him feel corrupt and dirty.

It didn't take long for Thomas to locate the source of the Dark Magic. He made good time coming up through the foothills and now stood on a cliff several hundred feet above a

Highland steppe laced with ravines and crevices on its northern face. Gusts of cold wind sent shivers through his body, so he unwrapped his dark green cloak and slipped it around his shoulders, securing it beneath his neck. After waiting a few minutes, a flash of movement below him caught his eye.

About a mile away a group of women and children exited the trees. Most walked hunched over, too tired to think, only concerned about where they placed their feet. They didn't bother to scout the surrounding countryside. No, he was wrong. There was a boy with them, leading the group along the floor of the ravine toward a pass that paralleled the steppe and led higher into the mountains. Large boy, rather. Though he was a mile or more away, with his heightened vision Thomas saw that this boy, who looked to be about his own age, was probably the same height as Rynlin with much broader shoulders. He too walked with weary steps, but that didn't stop him from glancing off to the sides every few seconds, looking for any movement. He must be the leader. If so, then it could mean only one thing.

Killeran's reivers had raided another village. These Highlanders had come a long way obviously, but unfortunately not far enough. The evil of the warlocks Thomas had been following approached rapidly from the same direction the weary troop had just come.

Thomas knelt down next to a cluster of rocks situated near the edge of the cliff. He would never get down there in time to help. Pounding his hand against the rock in frustration, he could only watch. He didn't have long to wait. Less than a minute later the pounding of horses' hooves echoed through the ravine. The boy knew exactly what was happening, but he had few options. Before he even saw his attackers, he ordered his people to scatter. A smart move on his part. Those who made it to the trees on either side would greatly improve their chances of escape. As his people ran for cover, the boy stood in the center of the ravine, his sword drawn.

The fastest of the Highlanders had reached the trees when the first reiver galloped into the ravine. Thomas sighed. A few would escape, but not many. They were just too tired, weighed down by the stress and fear they carried with them. The boy immediately placed himself in front of the reiver. It was a futile gesture, but one that Thomas admired. He certainly had courage.

The large boy never had a chance to make use of his sword. The horsemen avoided him and instead went after the women and children, the easiest prey. Recognizing what was happening, the boy ran toward one reiver who had jumped from his horse and grabbed the wrist of a woman clutching a small child to her breast. She struggled valiantly, just a few steps from the trees and freedom. The reiver never knew what hit him as the boy split his head in two, then gave the woman a push into the forest.

When the boy turned, another reiver charged toward him. The boy let out a yell that even Thomas could hear, a cry that tugged at his heart, that demanded that he do something! But he couldn't. Not yet. He had considered using the Talent, but there were at least three warlocks with this band of reivers, and even more in the general area. He was certain he could defeat the three, but it would weaken him greatly. If the other warlocks came upon him in such a state, he wouldn't stand a chance. He could offer no help now, but perhaps later. If the boy survived.

The reiver charging toward the boy stopped just out of his reach, and instead of pulling out a sword, pointed his hand at the boy. A warlock. Thomas felt the Dark Magic being manipulated in the ravine below. In seconds, the boy slumped to the ground unconscious. With the only threat removed, the reivers made quick work of the remaining Highlanders. Thomas guessed that half of the group reached the safety of the forest. A few of the reivers went after them, but they would have little luck finding them. At least the boy's brave stand wasn't in vain.

The reivers placed chains around the hands of the women and older children they had captured, not bothering with the youngest. Thomas saw the look of defeat on the captives' faces, their hope for freedom extinguished by the steel collars fixed around their necks and the long metal chain that attached one to the other. In only a few minutes it was over. The reivers headed back in the direction they had come with thirty captives trailing along behind them, with the boy tied to the back of the dead reiver's horse.

It was almost too much for Thomas to bear. This was his home, and his people! Thomas gripped the rocks in front of him, his knuckles white from the strain. He had to do something. He couldn't just sit there and watch. As the reivers disappeared from view, Thomas rose from his place on the cliff and trotted off to the northwest, paralleling their course. Tracking the reivers would be simple; just follow the evil of the warlocks.

Thomas matched his pace to that of his quarry, remaining well off to the west to prevent any chance of discovery. He stayed on his present course for several hours, until the sun began to drop in the sky. The reivers had stopped moving. Thomas wiped his forearm across his brow, removing some of the sweat that formed there. His pursuit had warmed him, so he again tied his cloak into a bundle and carried it across his back with his other supplies. He took a few sips from his water sack before stuffing everything except his sword under two large, column-like rocks, their tops balancing one another to form an oddly shaped entranceway.

He doubted the reivers he pursued would patrol this far to the west, but there was no reason to leave anything to chance. Thomas headed off into the forest, treading silently. Ari, one of his trainers, had spent many hours showing him how to walk across the forest floor without disturbing the branches, twigs or leaves. Thomas excelled at it. His grandfather once joked that Thomas could sneak up on the High King himself after walking five miles on dead branches and leaves, swipe the crown from his head and make his way back to where he started with no one the wiser. Rynlin wasn't far from the truth.

Thomas took his time as he approached. He could now hear clearly the reivers' voices. Though nothing was visible yet, it was louder than it should be. It sounded like this band of reivers had met up with another. The feeling of evil that Thomas had tracked came from just ahead. He continued to step forward on silent feet, then stopped.

Through the trees Thomas saw the campfires of the reivers, most of whom sat around them talking or eating. The prisoners were nowhere in sight, and that worried him. He was about to move closer when the crack of a twig off to his left froze his right foot just above the ground. Reluctant to make any motion, even moving his head just a fraction, Thomas instead used his peripheral vision to find the source of the noise.

A reiver stood off to his left, no more than ten feet away. The man leaned casually against a tree and spent more time looking in toward the camp, attracted by the activity at the fires, than outward. Thomas berated himself for not paying more attention to his surroundings. More foolishness on his part would do little to help the Highland captives and would most likely lead to his death.

That was something he wanted to avoid. He had a feeling that Rya's anger could transcend a simple obstacle such as death. Thomas was about to step backwards when he felt a tickle beneath his nose. The tickle quickly became almost unbearable. Thomas resisted the urge to scratch his upper lip with his finger, standing there for more than a minute, balanced on one foot, trying not to give in to his desire to sneeze. Thankfully the feeling faded away.

Then he smiled. If this guard was any model, the reivers

weren't expecting an attack. That was good. It would make his job easier. Much easier. Thomas looked a final time at the guard to his left before silently stepping backward, taking extra time to ensure absolute silence. A few minutes later he was well away from the camp.

He set off at a trot through the forest, going back to the strangely shaped rocks and pulling his travel bag from beneath them. He'd wait until it was early morning, when the guards struggled against sleep. Then the fun would begin.

24

SILENT APPROACH

The bright light of the full moon lit the reivers' camp as if it were early morning, offering a false sense of security to those within. The sentries had allowed the large cook fires to die down, until they were no more than smoldering ashes. Though the darkness dissipated somewhat, the shadows remained, and it was the shadows that Thomas skillfully used as he circled the camp.

He waited until well past midnight before silently reconnoitering the forest. The leader of this particular band of reivers had placed a ring of guards one hundred feet into the forest. Even with the trees to hide behind, Thomas saw them clearly in the moonlight and easily avoided them. Besides, at this time in the morning, most of the guards were too busy trying to stay awake. Rather than warning of potential danger, the quiet of the forest lulled them into a comfortable daze. Thomas had considered killing them, then discarded the idea. He didn't know when the guards changed. If the next set of reivers found the bodies, or didn't see the men they were to replace, before he left camp, then this escape would fail.

The reivers set up their camp just as Thomas had expected.

The cook fires formed a loose circle that served as the perimeter of the camp with squads of reivers curled up in their blankets around each one. A small cook fire segregated from the rest held a handful of sleeping men. Thomas assumed the warlocks stayed there, away from the others. Beyond the outer perimeter of fires and off to one side was a small tent. Whoever led the expedition probably slept there. On the other side a tiny, lonely fire flickered atop a small hillock. Several dozen bodies huddled around it. The women and children captured in the raid most likely.

After Thomas quietly passed through the outer ring of guards picketed in the forest, he stopped at the edge of the firelight and waited just within the trees. Most of the sentries were asleep, making his task that much easier. He stood there in the shadows for several more minutes, getting a feel for the tempo of the camp. The cool caress of the breeze felt good against his face. Despite the ease with which he passed through the picket line, on the inside his nerves threatened to get the better him, the cold sweat running down his back confirming it. Whoever led this raiding party was either much too confident or a fool. Having only a thin outer line of sentries was a huge mistake, and one that Thomas happily capitalized on.

Dropping to his stomach in the tall grass, Thomas entered the camp, dragging himself across the ground on his elbows and knees. The tall grass concealed him perfectly, and in a matter of minutes, he passed the cook fires and sleeping reivers and made his way into the center of the camp. The dew on the grass soaked through his clothes, and this time the cool breeze chilled him, but it was a small price to pay for his current success. Thomas remained where he was for several long minutes, looking for any sign of unexpected movement, listening for the wrong sound.

He considered the possible need for a diversion once he freed the captives so they could reach the forest safely. The easiest way to do that, of course, was to use the Talent. A few bolts of energy certainly would cause the panic required. Unfortunately, he couldn't chance it with a half dozen warlocks less than a hundred feet away. Not unless he was left with no other choice. As soon as Thomas drew on the Talent, the warlocks would know, and his great escape would become a grand failure.

No, he'd have to do it the hard way. First he needed the keys since the reivers had chained the women and children together. Again, he could use the Talent, but even the tiny amount of energy required to break the shackles could arouse the warlocks because of their proximity. Though the idea of taking on those lifeless bastards appealed to him, he had no right to further risk the lives of those he meant to free.

Satisfied that no one had stirred, Thomas pulled himself up and crouched low to the ground. Once he got past the campfires, he only had a short distance of open ground to cross to reach the prisoners. Moving back into the shadows of the darkened tent, he surveyed the open space before the hillock. Thomas jumped back in surprise as a dark shape loomed up in front of him.

"What the—"

Not giving the reiver time to finish his sentence, Thomas stabbed with his dagger. The sharp steel slid effortlessly between the links of the man's armor and found his heart. At the same time, Thomas clamped his hand over the man's mouth to prevent the reiver from screaming a warning. Thomas remained in that position until the man's strength gave out, sapped by the steel of the dagger. As the reiver's knees weakened, Thomas lowered him to the ground. He waited a full minute before removing his hand. Lifeless eyes stared back at him as he wiped his dagger on the man's sleeve. Thomas ignored the accusation he saw. After what they had done to his homeland, reivers deserved little sympathy. Thomas dragged the body behind the tent, thankful for the damp grass, which simplified his task.

Thomas smiled as he studied the scene before him. Another mistake. Thomas decided once and for all that whoever led this band of reivers was indeed a fool. The Highlanders were on a hillock that rose in the very center of their camp. On the one hand, Thomas understood why this site was chosen as a makeshift prison. The Highlanders were visible at all times to anyone in the camp, almost completely eliminating the opportunity for escape. But the reiver in command hadn't taken into account the possibility of help from the outside. A guard stood at each compass point, facing in toward the hillock. But, the guards couldn't see above the hillock, and therefore could not see one another. Their isolation would work to his advantage.

Thomas approached the first guard, whose back was turned. As he got closer, soft sounds of snoring drifted through the air. The reiver was using his spear to stay erect as he dozed. The man didn't stand a chance as Thomas came up from behind. Thomas slipped his dagger between the links of black chain mail and into his back while his hand snaked around and closed over the man's mouth to prevent a scream. With a final twist of the blade, the man crumpled to the ground. Thomas rifled through his uniform for the keys, but no luck.

He stepped on silent feet around the hillock to the next guard. The thick grass hid Thomas' approach, eliminating the sound of his footfalls as he hugged the earth. This reiver had not fallen asleep, but like his friend, stood facing the hillock. Thomas reached around the man in a smooth motion and sliced cleanly across his throat. He too fell to the ground, dead in seconds. This one also didn't have the keys. Thomas cursed silently. If neither one of the remaining guards had the keys, he'd have to make an uninvited visit to the man in the tent, which would complicate things greatly.

Thomas stepped around the base of the hillock and approached the third guard from behind, the thick grass again hiding his footsteps. Another quick sweep of his dagger across the man's throat and Thomas' task was almost complete. The keys were nowhere to be found, though. Thomas hoped that his luck wasn't running out. He glanced around to make sure that the camp was still silent before trotting through the high grass and coming around to the final guard.

Thomas began his approach from behind, moving slowly, silently, blending into his environment. He held his dagger loosely in his hand. After each kill he had wiped the blood onto the uniform of each guard. He didn't want it to drip down the blade onto his hand. Fergus Steelheart had taught him that, explaining how a young soldier had fought like a hero against the Golden Blades, killing several and displaying a remarkable ability with his sword.

Unfortunately for him, when he finally met Fergus in battle, he had not wiped his blade clean. The blood ran down the hilt and the sword slipped from his hand right when Fergus lunged forward with his own blade. Thomas certainly didn't want to repeat that experience. He was no more than twenty feet away from his final target when the guard abruptly turned around. Bored with his assignment of staring up at a dark hill, he just couldn't stand to look at it for a second longer.

The shock in the man's eyes at seeing Thomas standing there was mirrored in Thomas' at seeing the man turn around. Before the reiver could shout a warning, Thomas adjusted the grip on his dagger, taking the point in his fingers. In one smooth motion he cocked his arm and released. The dagger took the last guard in the throat. The man feebly tried to remove it as his blood poured out onto the earth, but his fingers were already growing weak. The reiver slumped to the ground, the shock still in his eyes. A soft gurgle rose from his lips as his last breath left his body, lost in the soft brush of the wind across the grass.

Thomas rushed forward and searched the man's pockets. He smiled as his hand closed around a steel ring of keys. Perhaps his luck had not yet left him. Taking the keys, he looked around a final time. The camp remained quiet. If all continued to go well, the reivers would never know he had been there until he and the Highlanders were leagues away. Confident of his impending success, Thomas started up the hill as the moon moved lazily across the sky. A few more hours of darkness remained. By the time the sun rose, he'd have these people well on their way to the higher passes where the reivers dared not follow.

25

DISCOVERY

Killeran tried to sleep in his bed for several hours, but with little success. Something bothered him, he just didn't know what. Maybe it was the almost total failure of the morning raid. He needed more miners, desperately, and he could not afford many more mistakes. If he didn't increase production Rodric would be the least of his concerns. Dinnegan had taken a personal interest in the success of their business venture, and the memories of their last meeting stayed with him. He hated the man, hated him with a passion, but he also envied him. Of course, at the moment, he was in no position to do anything about it.

Killeran threw his covers to the ground and sat up on the bed, swinging his legs onto the rug that covered the grass of the glade. He hastily pulled on his boots and draped a cloak over his shoulders. As he headed for the tent flap, he strapped on his sword. There was little reason to lie here and do nothing. Over the years he had developed the habit of inspecting his men at odd hours. It helped to keep them on their toes. Besides, maybe his doing something would alleviate his worry.

As he walked out into the early morning, he was greeted by

a gust of cold wind that slipped underneath his open cloak and chilled his entire body. He pulled his cloak closer around himself, muttering and wiping his nose on his sleeve. This blasted, never-ending cold was making his life miserable. As he walked away from the tent, the day's events played through his mind. He couldn't believe how poorly his men had performed during the raid. He had set his trap perfectly, but it disintegrated in a matter of minutes. As a result, he had come away with two dozen women and children and one boy.

He could certainly put them to work in the mines, but they wouldn't last long and would produce very little in the way of gold or precious minerals. He needed the men. They lived longer in the severe conditions of the mines, if only because of their stubbornness. When he returned to his main camp he'd make an example of someone. He couldn't afford their blunders anymore. Such a display always did wonders in terms of the effort put forth by his men.

Killeran made his way into the forest, checking his outer ring of defenses first. He was pleased to see that his sentries were awake at their posts despite the hour. He had expected to find at least one sleeping soundly. A part of him was disappointed. He liked nothing more than putting someone in his place.

Several of the men in this raiding party had served under him for many years. They knew his habits and remembered what he had done to the last man he found sleeping at his post. Stories like that traveled fast among his troops. Killeran believed that fear was all you needed to be a great general. He had proven that time and again. Fear. Respect did nothing for you. With fear, you could achieve anything. Perhaps that was the problem. Perhaps his men did, indeed, need another lesson. He smiled at the thought.

He returned to the camp a half-hour later and walked toward the hillock, wanting to check the sentries stationed there before returning to his cot. Maybe he could get a few hours of sleep before morning after all. Then he could make an example of someone. It would serve two purposes really: improve the performance of his men and sufficiently cow his prisoners to take away any thought of escape during the long trek back to the fort. Killeran grinned wickedly. Besides, it would be fun.

He was almost there when his foot caught on something and he fell flat on his face. Killeran landed heavily on the ground, unable to break his fall with his arms, which were trapped in the folds of his cloak.

"What the bloody—" Killeran continued to mutter to himself as he slowly rose to his feet, rubbing the aching shoulder that had absorbed most of the impact from his fall. He had just found his latest example. When he located the man responsible for leaving his pack here, he'd make certain it never happened again.

Wait. Killeran examined the bundle that he had tripped over more closely. It was oddly shaped and didn't resemble the standard packs his reivers carried. He knelt down to get a better look. Killeran jumped back a few paces, the bile rising in his throat. He had tripped over one of his men, dead from a knife to the heart. His sword was in his hand in an instant. Reivers were typically violent, and when arguments developed, they often ended in bloodshed. So finding a dead man in the morning wasn't always a surprise, but the kills were never as clean as this.

His feeling of foreboding returned. This could be nothing more than another argument between some of his men gone sour. Then again, maybe not. Killeran trotted toward the hillock, scanning the camp for any sign of movement as he did so. Reaching the base of the small hill, he only heard the swishing of the wind through the tall grass. He had left four men here. None were in sight. Something was wrong, terribly wrong. Making a quick circuit around the hill, Killeran still couldn't find his men. Clutching the hilt of his sword tightly in his hand, he started up the slope. It might be nothing at all. Instead of one lesson for tomorrow, there would be four. Then again, it could be something else entirely.

26

BAD LUCK

Thomas reached the top of the hill in only a few seconds, the small fire having almost burnt out. As a result, the women had gathered all the children together to keep them warm, lying in a tight circle. They had fallen asleep easily, the fear and exhaustion of the past day getting the better of them. The boy was off to the side, his face bruised and his lower lip cut. Thomas had expected worse. The reivers certainly weren't known for being gentle, especially when you killed one of their friends.

Thomas moved on silent feet to the sleeping form. When the boy breathed he wheezed through his nose. Probably broken. Thomas knelt down and covered the boy's mouth with his hand.

In an instant the boy came awake, struggling to get up. Thomas pressed him back down, keeping his hand over his mouth. The heavy chains on his ankles and wrists forced the boy to be still. He was more surprised than anything else, as Thomas didn't resemble a reiver. The bastards had grown tired of beating on him as soon as dinner was ready, leaving him there to his misery.

Oso took solace in the fact that half of his people had escaped to safety during the attack in the ravine. The fact that the other half was stuck there with him on this hill trying not to freeze to death ate at his insides. He blamed himself for that, though Lara and the other women in the group had told him that he shouldn't, that he had done the best he could. That only made him feel worse. His best wasn't good enough, which in his eyes made him a failure. This surprise visitor might give him a chance to make amends.

Thomas dangled the keys before the large boy's eyes, asking with his eyebrows if he understood what was about to happen. Oso nodded that he did. Thomas made quick work of the locks, helping the boy remove the chains from around his wrists and ankles. Oso gratefully rubbed some feeling back into his limbs.

"Wake the others and keep them quiet. Once we've removed the locks, we'll take them that way into the trees."

Oso nodded and crawled over to Lara, who lay with a small child against her. The child shivered in the cold. Oso squeezed his hands together in frustration. A child shouldn't suffer like this. The stranger had pointed to the side of the camp farthest away from the warlocks with the fewest campfires, which meant fewer reivers to pass. Oso hoped desperately that their luck held.

Thomas followed after the boy, who moved gingerly on limbs still getting used to the increased flow of blood. He unlocked the clasps around the Highlanders' necks and wrists as quietly and as fast as he could after Oso had awakened them, motioning each time for the person to remain silent. The women were freed first and then gathered the children together, rubbing their own and the children's wrists to get the blood flowing again.

Thomas moved among them, seeing where the steel had cut into the skin of the Highlanders. As he freed each person, his anger grew. You didn't treat children this way! You didn't treat anyone this way! Thomas' blood began to boil. He reached the last woman, who waited impatiently for him to release her. In a second, he was done. The Highlanders were free. Now all they had to do was make it into the forest. The boy had already gotten everyone together, each woman looking after a child.

Thomas spun when he heard a foot crunch on the hardened earth of the hill. A man with a remarkably large nose appeared at the top of the hillock, his sword drawn.

"Who are you?" the rat-faced man asked in shock.

Thomas' response surprised him even more. Thomas leaped to his feet and charged toward the man, catching him in the chest with his shoulder. The reiver flew back through air over the side of the hillock. Thomas didn't bother to watch the soldier fall. Instead, he looked for the boy.

"Down the other side. Now!"

The boy started off immediately, scrabbling down the hillside, the women right on his heels. They were just as anxious to be away as he was. Thomas waited until the last Highlander had started down before going himself. He hoped whoever that was had broken his neck in the fall. It would make his task that much easier. When he reached the bottom of the hill, Thomas ran over to where one of the dead sentries lay. He reached down and pulled the reivers' sword from his scabbard, then handed it to the boy. The boy nodded his gratitude.

"Let's get these people moving. We don't have much time." The boy didn't bother to respond, instead leading the way through the still sleeping camp with his people following behind him. He, too, sensed the urgency of the situation.

Killeran survived his fall with no more than a few bumps and bruises. After he hit the ground, he struggled with his cloak for several seconds, as the white cloth tangled his legs during the fall. Finally, he freed himself and ran over to where his sword had landed. That boy had the nerve to sneak into his camp and then attack him! A boy! Now he'd pay the price for his audacity.

"Reivers awake! To me! Reivers to me!"

27

EASY DECISION

Killeran's shout blasted like a trumpet through the night, setting off an explosion of activity. Most of the reivers were still too dazed by sleep to realize what was going on. Nevertheless, they assumed that they were under attack, and since the most natural direction would be from the trees, they grabbed their weapons and rushed off to defend the perimeter.

The confusion worked to Thomas' advantage as he and Oso led the Highlanders through the camp. They quickly dispatched the few reivers still around the campfires, either too slow or not wanting to follow their comrades. Some of the Highland women relieved the dead men of their weapons. When the reivers tried to capture them again, they'd have a much harder time of it.

Unfortunately, the confusion only lasted for a few minutes. Thomas and Oso had almost reached the trees when they ran into six reivers. The two threw themselves at the black-armored men with a vengeance, their anger driving their sword arms at blazing speeds. Though outnumbered, it didn't matter. The skirmish didn't last long, but the sounds of battle drew the attention of the other reivers, who quickly realized their mistake.

"Into the woods," Thomas yelled. "Run! Into the woods!"

The Highlanders didn't need to be told twice. The women dashed forward, the children in tow, disappearing among the trees. Several reivers tried to follow in pursuit, but Thomas and the large boy remained behind, blocking their path. They had succeeded, at least in part.

"You, too," said Thomas to the boy. "Into the woods."

"No. You risked your life for me. Now I can repay you." Thomas glanced over at the tall boy, his face swollen, his wrists cut by the shackles. There was a fierce pride in his eyes, and a sense of duty. "Besides, it's too late."

The boy was right. The reivers had surrounded them. The boy moved behind Thomas, watching his back for him. The reivers seemed reluctant to press forward. The handiwork of these two boys lay at their feet. They had killed a half dozen reivers already, and those around them didn't want to risk their lives as well. Better to wait for the warlocks.

"What are you waiting for?" snarled Killeran as he finally located the source of all his trouble, following the clash of steel on steel. Half his men were still running around in circles, defending against an enemy that wasn't there.

"I want the big one alive," he ordered. "The green-eyed boy is mine."

The reivers surged forward. One reiver immediately fell to the ground dead, Thomas' sword finding his heart. Another fell an instant later, a victim of the large boy's blade. The reivers became even more wary and reluctant, hesitating with their attacks despite Killeran's presence. The fight continued for several minutes, Thomas and the boy back to back. Though they had known each other for only a few minutes, they sensed each other's movements as they circled around, defending themselves and each other. It was as if they had known each other all their lives.

Killeran waited impatiently, urging his men to attack all at once. Finally the strategy paid off. After a half-dozen more reivers appeared, the group charged forward, forcing Thomas and the boy to fight off as many as three blades at a time. The injuries of the previous day began to wear on the boy, and though he remained a deadly opponent, his movements slowed dramatically. A reiver finally got past his defenses, stabbing his blade into the boy's sword arm.

Thomas tried to help him, but was too busy fending off his own attackers. Suddenly, they were gone. The reivers that stood before him stepped back, instead forming a ring around the boy. Thomas was about to try forcing his way through, but instead he dove to the ground, barely avoiding the blade of the man he had knocked down the hill. He was on his feet again in an instant.

"You have done well, boy. But your luck is about to run out."

The man looked familiar to Thomas. How could that be? Thomas had little time to ponder it. The man lunged forward, trying to skewer Thomas with his blade. He easily avoided the thrust, dancing to the side. Thomas glanced behind him and saw that his friend was still surrounded by reivers, who made no move toward him yet. The boy was tiring, that much was obvious. If Thomas wanted to escape he'd have to do it soon, otherwise they'd never have another opportunity. The initial confusion that worked to their advantage in the beginning would not last for much longer. The man lunged forward again with his blade and Thomas stepped out of the way.

This man with the large nose was beginning to irritate him. He lunged again with his sword, aiming for Thomas' gut. Thomas dodged to the side, but this time returned with a thrust of his own, catching the man by surprise. Off balance, the ratlike man barely avoided the blade. He couldn't stop his forward motion, though, and fell to the ground heavily for the second time in an hour. He tried to rise but stopped, cold steel pressed against his throat.

Looking up, he saw the boy staring down at him. His eyes were hard, harder than they should be for a boy. A bolt of fear settled in the bottom of Killeran's stomach. He came to the horrible realization that he had misjudged this boy, thinking that his youth would limit his skill with a blade. The boy's green eyes flashed in anger and Killeran felt the steel pressed harder against his throat. A warm trickle ran down his neck. Those cold green eyes held no mercy, only death.

"Drop your blade, boy, or your friend dies."

Thomas looked over his shoulder, his sword pressed tightly against the man's throat. The Highland boy had put up a good fight, but his exhaustion had done him in. Four reivers lay dead at his feet. But two now held him by the arms, while the third, a grizzled veteran, held a dagger to his throat.

"I said drop the sword, boy." To exclamate his point Kursool pushed the dagger against the boy's throat. A few drops of dark red blood welled up and dripped slowly down the boy's neck, staining his already ragged shirt.

Thomas looked down at his prisoner. The man hadn't said a word, but his fear was plain. The eyes always told all. They were filled with stark terror, and Thomas noticed that the man's body was shaking slightly. He knew that killing this man would be a good thing. He was obviously the leader of this band of reivers. His gleaming silver breastplate, now dented in several places, and his once swan white cloak, now muddied and torn, testified to that.

He turned his gaze to the boy, who stood there still as a rock, held by two reivers and the blade against his neck. There was no fear there. Only duty. The boy could have escaped with the others, and in fact should have. But he had stayed behind and tried to help Thomas prevent the reivers from following.

Thomas locked eyes with the boy. There was courage there, and loyalty. His eyes said that Thomas was free to kill this man — should kill the man — and the boy wouldn't blame him for his own death. An almost imperceptible whimper issued from the man beneath his blade. He could not sacrifice a man of courage for a coward.

Thomas removed his blade from the man's neck and let his sword drop to the ground. The man he had held hostage let out a sigh of relief, then quickly regained his composure. Three reivers rushed forward, knocking Thomas to the ground and holding him there. Thomas didn't resist. The boy still had a knife pressed against his throat. Thomas hoped his sacrifice was worth it.

"Thank you, Kursool," said Killeran, as he bent over and reclaimed his sword, slipping it back into his scabbard. He tried to recapture a measure of his dignity, but failed miserably. His body still shook slightly from fear. The man turned toward Thomas. "As I said, boy, your luck has run out." The man motioned to one of the soldiers holding him down, who then rapped Thomas on the side of the head with the hilt of his dagger. Darkness quickly consumed him.

Killeran examined the now unconscious whelp. "Chain these two and double the guard."

The sergeant who had recaptured the large boy stepped forward. "Should we pursue the Highlanders, my lord?"

Killeran glared at him. "No, they're not worth the effort. Besides, if there are more of them out there like this one," motioning to Thomas' limp form, "we'd only be asking for more trouble. No, I think it's time we return to the fort."

The sergeant nodded, then went off yelling for more chains and shackles.

Killeran felt the need to be behind solid walls, surrounded by his men. Death had brushed just a little too close for his taste this time. He stood there for a moment, watching his men fasten a steel collar around the boy's throat, then run a length of chain through the ring. At least he'd have some entertainment over the next few days. This boy with the green eyes intrigued him. He'd have to learn more about this one before he killed him.

THE END

Keep reading for the first three chapters of Book 3, *The Raptor of the Highlands.*

BONUS MATERIAL

If you really enjoyed this story, I need you to do me a HUGE favor – please follow me on Amazon and BookBub.

And if you have a few minutes, consider writing a review.

Keep reading for the first three chapters of Book 3 of *The Sylvan Chronicles, The Raptor of the Highlands.*

PETER WACHT

THE RAPTOR OF THE HIGHLANDS

The Raptor of the Highlands

By Peter Wacht

Book 3 of The Sylvan Chronicles

Published in the United States by Kestrel Media Group LLC.

ISBN: 978-1-950236-04-6

eBook ISBN: 978-1-950236-05-3

Library of Congress Control Number: 2019905673

❀ Created with Vellum

1. A FRIEND

The dreams swept through his mind like a tidal wave. In the first, he stood on a huge promontory looking out over a drop of a thousand feet. The wind tugged at him, wanting to pull him to his death, but he resisted. Power coursed within him. He held the Sword of the Highlands above his head in triumph, and for the first time he felt free — and in control of his own destiny.

That dream disintegrated, replaced by another. He stood in the middle of a pit with soft, white sand beneath his feet. The walls of the pit, twenty feet high and made of a glassy stone, appeared impossible to climb. He gripped a spear in his hand, but it was like none he had ever seen before. It resembled a quarterstaff, but even that term wasn't quite right because of the long, sharp blades affixed to its ends. Blood covered his body; some of it his own, most of it not.

He couldn't remember what had happened, but again he experienced a momentary thrill of exultation. He had won. He had survived! This time, though, that feeling disappeared when his gaze traveled out of the pit to the stands situated around it, where lords and ladies watched him, looks of surprise and wonder on their faces. His eyes went from one arrogant or fearful expression to the next, until he stopped at one. The girl. The girl from the Burren. Kaylie. Instead of feeling happy at seeing her beautiful, blue eyes, though, he felt betrayed. Betrayed by her.

Another dream entered his mind, pushing the other one out. He knelt on a windswept slope, the gritty black dirt staining his breeks. It was daytime, but the dark, churning clouds created a perpetual dusk. Blackened mountains towered above him. The wind twisted and turned around the peaks, carrying fragments of sound. He concentrated as best he could, but found it difficult. He was tired. His energy almost gone. He had been searching for something, something that would allow him to escape the cold, the fear. But he had failed. The Key was now beyond his grasp.

Finally, after several frustrating minutes, the fragments of sound became words in his ears, the whispers teasing him, pushing at the bounds of his sanity. He tried to fight it, to hold back the madness seeping into his brain, but he could struggle for only so long. He fell forward in the black dirt, a dark haze covering his mind. The words finally made sense: *The shadow rules. The shadow rules. Death to those who oppose the shadow.* As the darkness swept him away, he knew that he would never wake again.

The dreams came faster and faster, speeding through his mind, making it impossible for him to remember them all. He knew they were important, that they affected his life in some way. If only he could decipher them and find out what messages they contained. But the dreams only increased in speed, swirling around in his head like a tornado. He wanted to escape, to flee from his own mind, but he didn't know how. Then the dreams disappeared, replaced by a bright light.

Thomas enjoyed the calm and quiet after enduring the whirlwind in his head. Slowly, the light grew stronger, forcing his eyes open. His head exploded in pain. He pushed himself up to a seated position, squinting because of the bright sunlight and rubbing the side of his head with his hand. At least he tried to. The shackles on his wrists prevented it. With some careful maneuvering, he was finally able to do it. A lump had formed there, just above the ear. Other than that, he was fine, except, of course, for the tremendous headache. Then he remembered everything.

He had tried to help that group of Highlanders the reivers had captured, and though he had succeeded in freeing them, he now faced the same predicament himself. His grandfather had been right. Eventually the risks would catch up to him, and in this particular instance they had. He hated when Rynlin was right! At least he wouldn't have to see the look of smugness his grandfather so enjoyed giving him. Actually, considering his present circumstances, that look of smugness probably wouldn't be so bad.

Opening his eyes fully, he winced. The early morning sun had not yet burned off the dew from the grass, which helped to explain why his shirt and breeks were damp. He turned his head from side to side, surveying his position. He was in the middle of the reivers' camp, or what was left of it anyway. Most of the reivers had formed into a long line of two horseman abreast, while a few struggled to pull down the tent.

"Good morning."

Thomas shifted around slowly, gasping for breath because of the sharp pain that shot through his head from the movement. The pounding in his head increased. The large boy stared back at him, his face a mass of welts and bruises, his long blond hair matted down by blood and dirt. He had tied a strip of cloth around the wound on his right arm. The boy looked to be his own age, though he was massive. Thomas felt like a dwarf sitting there across from him. His surrender had served a

purpose at least. The reivers hadn't killed the Highlander —
yet.

"How long have I been out?"

"Two hours," replied the boy.

Thomas grunted in reply. Two hours. It had felt like an eter-
nity. And those dreams. They were important. He needed to
remember them. But he couldn't. Bits and pieces flirted with his
memory, but the puzzle refused to form.

"How's your arm?"

The large boy grunted. "As good as can be expected. Just a
scratch really."

"You should have escaped when you had the chance," said
Thomas, gingerly rubbing at his head. He had to do it carefully,
otherwise he might hit himself in the head with the chains
attached to the shackles, and his headache was bad enough
already.

"I know. But I couldn't let you have all the fun. It wouldn't
have been fair." The boy looked at the eight reivers stationed
around them with hate-filled eyes.

"Well, that explains everything," said Thomas.

The boy smiled. "Thank you for freeing my people. A debt
is owed. Whenever you have need, it will be repaid."

Thomas was going to tell him that it wasn't necessary, that
there was no need to repay the debt. The intensity in the boy's
eyes made him think better of it. He had been away from his
people for a long time and forgotten some of the customs. This
one came back to him quickly. If one Highlander made a
personal sacrifice for the benefit of another Highlander, such as
a Marcher saving another Marcher's life, the person would say,
"A debt is owed." Men of honor did not scoff at such a statement, as it was never said lightly.

"When I have need," replied Thomas, remembering the
correct response.

The boy nodded. "You look like a Highlander, but then again, you don't."

It was a strange thing to say, but Thomas understood. "I am a Highlander. My mother wasn't."

The large boy nodded again. He studied Thomas critically for a few moments. "You fight well, green eyes. My name is Kylin, but my friends call me Oso."

"A strong name, Oso. My name is Thomas."

"That, too, is a strong name. Well met, Thomas."

Oso tried to extend his hand in greeting, but the chains held him back.

"So, the two young heroes are awake," said Killeran, walking past the eight guards and standing over them. "Good. It is time to go to your new home, or rather what will serve as your home until you die."

Killeran thought that the last portion of his statement would register with the two. They were young, with long lives ahead of them, or rather they did before their capture. But they ignored him, giving him only steely glances. He couldn't tell which one wanted him dead the most -- the large one or the one with green eyes. Green eyes? Why did that tug at his memory? He tried to remember for a moment, then gave up.

"You have cost me twenty able-bodied workers, and more than a dozen reivers, so it looks like you will have to do the work of all. No matter. You'll simply die sooner."

Killeran studied his two new prisoners, still expecting a reaction. But there wasn't one. They were still proud, still confident. By the end of the day, though, he'd have them blubbering like children.

"Bring them," he said, motioning to the reivers.

The reivers half-dragged, half-carried Thomas and Oso to the end of the two cavalry columns, then affixed long chains to their collars. Two reivers at the end of the column grasped the leashes.

The reivers then placed chains around their ankles, with a two-foot length attached to their leg shackles. They would have a very hard time going faster than a slow walk, as neither could extend their legs more than a foot at a time. Of course, Killeran didn't plan for them to walk very far at all. These two boys intrigued him, and the one with green eyes moreso than the other. Why? Why should that bother him so? He shook his head in frustration.

Killeran wiped his sleeve across his nose. His cold hadn't gotten any better. If he had to suffer through another miserable day in this inhospitable land, then these two could do so in a slightly different way. Satisfied that his prisoners were prepared for the day's journey back into the foothills, Killeran walked up to the front of the column and climbed onto his horse. Cutting the air sharply with his arm, the column started forward.

They had traveled for no more than a few minutes before he heard a satisfying sound that made him smile. Turning in his saddle, he saw that the large boy had tripped over a rock and was having a hard time getting up again because of the chains. He was dragged a short distance before he finally regained his feet. It looked like it just might be a very good day. Later in the morning he would pick up the pace and let the horses stretch their legs. Yes, it would be a very good day indeed.

2. A DRAG

Thomas tasted dirt for the twentieth time that day. Spitting the grainy particles out of his mouth, he glanced at his companion sharing in the misery. Oso looked just as bad as Thomas felt. His body demanded that he stop and lay there for the next ten years. Every muscle burned, every bone ached. He ignored the pain and forced himself to rise as quickly as he could, not wanting to get dragged across the rocky soil again. The chains around his ankles weighed him down, impeding his efforts.

He stumbled for the first few yards as he struggled to maintain his balance and resume the awkward gait the chains required. The reiver holding on to the leash attached to his collar didn't care about Thomas' struggles. In fact, he rather enjoyed them, putting heel to horse whenever he fell to make things just a little more difficult. And this was the easy part, when the horses moved at a walk. Trying to keep pace with the column at a trot with a short length of chain attached to your ankles just didn't work. Once you fell down, you couldn't get back up. All you could do was try to avoid the larger rocks or stones that his guard had a particular knack for finding.

They had traveled since early morning, Killeran very intent

upon getting somewhere fast and not allowing anything to slow him down. Several times during the day he had ridden to the back of the column to check on them. Each time afterward he quickened the column's pace, taking a special glee in the two boys' constant falls.

Thomas again looked over at Oso, who trudged along beside him. Oso's size was intimidating, but he was remarkably quick and agile for one so big. Nevertheless, he had spent a lot more time getting dragged behind his jailer's horse than Thomas had behind his, and it showed. Now the rest of his body matched his face, covered in welts and bruises and cuts. The wound on his arm had reopened. His clothes were torn in a dozen places and he was caked in mud and dirt. Thomas knew his condition was just as bad. On the bright side, though, his headache was gone. In fact, that was the only part of his body that didn't hurt at the moment.

He wondered what Rya would have done if he had come home looking like this. He smiled to himself thinking about it. She'd probably have a fit. Thomas pushed the thought from his mind. He didn't have time to think about that. He needed to find a way to escape, yet all he could do at the moment was concentrate on his feet. If his chains got tangled, he'd never get back up. At least it was getting dark. Soon they'd have to stop, then Thomas could concentrate on escaping.

3. IGNORED TAUNTS

Evening reluctantly gave way to night, and Thomas was thankful for the opportunity to rest. His entire body hurt. The reivers who served as their jailers had dragged Thomas and Oso into the middle of the camp where a lone tree stood in the center of the clearing. Suddenly, Thomas fell forward, landing hard on the ground. Thomas' jailer grinned after having kicked him in the small of his back. The other reiver produced a chain and wrapped it around the trunk of the tree, then affixed it to their chains as well.

Oso dropped to the ground next to Thomas, leaning against the tree. They were completely exhausted. Neither had a drop of energy left. It was several minutes before either could speak, and even then it was through gasps for breath.

"So, do I look as bad as I feel?" asked Oso, stretching his long legs out in front of him. His muscles screamed in protest, but he ignored them. He readjusted the strip of cloth and tightened it around his arm. That should stop the bleeding.

"Worse," replied Thomas. He wasn't as winded as Oso. He had Rynlin and Rya to thank for that. His constant training had helped him greatly during the day's ordeal.

Oso tried to laugh, and instead it came out as a wheeze, finding it difficult while catching his breath. He sounded like Tigan, an old man in his village who laughed so hard that sometimes his face turned a bright red from the lack of air.

"So how's your head?"

"It's the least of my worries right now," replied Thomas. "And your arm?"

"Like you, the least of my worries."

"Well, it was a pleasant day nonetheless," said Thomas, finding that talking helped to take his mind away from the bolts of pain that shot through his legs. He tried to stretch them out but had to stop halfway. They were cramping up, the sharp pain reawakening his senses. He'd try again in a few minutes. "A warm sun. A pleasant breeze. It's always nice to be outside on a day like this."

Oso looked over at his new friend as if something had been rattled in the smaller boy's head during one of his falls.

Thomas explained himself. "It helps to take away the ache when your mind focuses on something else."

Oso nodded, then tried it himself. He imagined that he was back near his village, stalking a large buck that had wondered close to his hiding place. In absolute silence, he affixed an arrow to his bow and stepped out from between two large trees. He stepped slowly through the brush, careful not to disturb anything that would give him away to his quarry. It was good to hunt again. To feel the rush of adrenaline as you closed in for the kill. He just needed to get a little closer. Just a little closer. He pulled back the bow, the string almost touching his face. Just a little closer.

A sharp pain shot through Oso's leg, jolting him from his reverie. The buck dashed off into the woods before he could release his arrow.

"Time to eat, boy," said one of the reivers. "Now take the bowl this time or I'll break your leg."

Oso stared back at the reiver, hate welling up in his eyes. Still, he took the bowl. He needed to eat, to keep his strength up, otherwise he'd never escape. Oso held the bowl to his nose, sniffing at the contents. Some kind of stew, he decided. It didn't smell very good, but he really didn't have a choice. He gobbled it down quickly. His stomach growled for more, but he doubted he'd get any. Thomas had also finished his meal, and now lay back against the tree. His eyes closed, Oso wondered if he actually slept.

"No, just resting," said Thomas.

"How did you know—"

"It was nothing," said Thomas, opening his eyes and leaning forward. He quickly examined what was going on around them. The reivers had formed their camp in a circle, with the tree as its center. Eight reivers guarded them. Either Killeran was a wary man or one frightened easily by two boys. "It seems that we are quite popular this evening."

"Yes, it does seem that way, doesn't it," said Oso. "We should be honored, I guess, having eight nursemaids." Oso's voice rose so the guards could hear. "Two boys and eight nursemaids."

Though every part of him hurt, Oso knew what Thomas was thinking. Escape. He was thinking it as well. But they wouldn't succeed if eight guards stood around them all night. Maybe some would grow bored with their duty, and Oso's words would be remembered. Some of the reivers might find something better to do than guard two boys and slip away for a few hours, giving them a chance.

"Remarkable, isn't it," said Thomas. "We're tied to a tree by our necks, and our arms and legs are chained together, yet still we garner this much attention. You know, Oso, we really should be honored."

The guards didn't appear to be paying attention to them, but Thomas knew that they could hear their chatter. They might be wasting their time in idle conversation at the moment, but they had nothing to lose. Besides, it might work. Fewer eyes meant more of a chance at freedom.

"Stop the chatter or you'll be dead boys," said Kursool, who came striding toward them from the direction of Killeran's tent. The sergeant was a broad man. Thomas judged that with his massive shoulders he was wide enough for two men. As a result, his legs looked tiny, which made his whole body appear disproportionate.

The sergeant stopped right in front of them. Unexpectedly, he lashed out with his leg, striking Oso across the chin. The blow sent him reeling. The only thing that kept him from falling to the grass was the chain around his neck. Oso fought against the pain, the blow having reawakened all of his injuries earned during his early morning struggle with the reivers. He refused to cry out, though. He would not show any sign of weakness to this bastard. Slowly, he pulled himself back up, until he lay back against the trunk. If not for the tree, he wouldn't have had the strength to hold himself up.

Kursool nodded in satisfaction, pleased with the effects of his blow. He then turned his attention to the other boy and was about to deliver another kick when his eyes caught Thomas'. It was full dark now and Thomas' eyes glowed brightly. They resembled green fire, mirroring the anger contained within him. The sergeant knew what Thomas was thinking. He knew it in his heart. If the boy was free, the sergeant would already be dead. Kursool was not accustomed to fear. He had seen much in his life, having fought in many campaigns, but he had never seen anything like this. He took a step back from the tree.

"You," he said, motioning to one of the reivers standing guard. "Unlock the small one. Lord Killeran wants to see him." The reiver rushed forward, eager to do the sergeant's bidding. He twisted the key in the lock holding the chain around Thomas' neck, then pulled him to his feet. Thomas realized that his plans for escape would have to wait. As the sergeant and the reiver dragged him across the ground, a sense of foreboding filled him.

I hope you enjoyed the first three chapters. To keep reading *The Raptor of the Highlands,* Book 3 of *The Sylvan Chronicles*, you can order your copy from my website or Amazon.

www.PeterWachtBooks.com

This short story is a prelude to the events in my series *The Tales of Caledonia* and is free to readers who receive my newsletter.

Join Peter's newsletter and get your FREE short story at www.PeterWachtBooks.com.